THE NANCY DREW FILES™

A Summer of Love Trilogy #2

Case 49

PORTRAIT IN CRIME

CAROLYN KEENE

AN ARCHWAY PAPERBACK
Published by POCKET BOOKS
New York   London   Toronto   Sydney   Tokyo   Singapore

AN ARCHWAY PAPERBACK *Original*

An Archway Paperback published by
POCKET BOOKS, a division of Simon & Schuster Inc.
1230 Avenue of the Americas, New York, NY 10020

ISBN: 0-671-70026-X

First Archway Paperback printing July 1990

10 9 8 7 6 5 4 3 2 1

Printed in the U.S.A.

IL 7+

Chapter

One

I LOVE FEELING the ocean breeze on my face," Bess Marvin said, shouting over the drone of the powerboat's engine. She was standing in the stern, her blond hair pulled neatly back in a ponytail. "Let's spend every summer at the beach!"

Nancy Drew's blue eyes sparkled as she leaned her head to her friend's ear. "I know why you're so happy," she teased in a low voice, casting her eyes in the direction of the good-looking blond guy at the steering wheel. "And it has nothing to do with the ocean breeze and the beach!"

"Nancy!" Bess's pretty face turned pink. "Tommy's just a friend," she said in a whisper so Tommy couldn't possibly hear.

1

Nancy stretched her long tanned legs on the padded seat and smiled. Bess had jumped at the chance to go waterskiing the minute Tommy Gray had suggested it. Then she'd dragged her cousin, George Fayne, and Nancy all over the Hamptons for two days shopping for the sleek pink bathing suit she was wearing. One thing was for sure, Nancy knew. Bess's enthusiasm wasn't out of any love of the sport. Bess avoided exercise every chance she could!

Nancy, Bess, and George had come to the Hamptons to spend a relaxing summer with Nancy's aunt, Eloise Drew. They'd had a lot of fun, Nancy thought, but they hadn't had much time for relaxation. The first couple of weeks had been great, full of new friends and, for George, a new romance. The three girls had spent lazy days on the beach and nights out dancing. Then they were suddenly plunged into a mystery. Now, Nancy mused, it was time for relaxing.

"Tommy's a really great guy, though," Bess said, moving Nancy's legs to sit beside her. As the girls were gazing at his sun-bleached hair, Tommy turned his freckled face toward them and gave Bess a smile.

"Don't you think he's cute, Nancy?" Bess asked. "I mean, he's not glamorous like Sasha . . ." Her voice trailed off.

No, Nancy agreed, glancing over at the lithe, handsome Sasha Petrov, who was leaning against the rail near Tommy. Not many teenagers were

2

like Sasha. The nineteen-year-old Russian was one of a kind.

Sasha was one of the lead dancers at an international dance institute that had been set up in the Hamptons as part of a summer cultural program. The institute had brought together some of the most talented young dancers from all over the world.

Nancy's aunt Eloise was Sasha's local sponsor, and she'd asked Nancy and her friends to take him around during his free time. That was easy enough. The tough part was that Sasha had begun flirting with Nancy the minute they met. So far, he had honored her request to be just friends, but Nancy still hadn't figured out how she felt about *him*.

She shrugged. "Sasha's fun," she said neutrally, "when he's not following your every step."

"You mean, when he's not following *your* every step." Bess grinned. "We found out long ago that he's interested only in a certain red-haired detective. You know you love it, too."

Nancy felt her face getting hot. These days, Sasha seemed to pop up whenever he wasn't in rehearsal. Nancy had been seeing a lot of him lately—and she had been enjoying it, she had to admit.

"Speaking of following someone around, can you believe George passed up waterskiing?" Bess commented. "She would have had a blast today."

"Well, Gary had an early-morning test flight,

3

and I guess they decided to do something by themselves the rest of the day," Nancy replied.

Bess tossed her head. "They spend every minute together! It's a good thing George isn't always in love. We'd never see her!"

As soon as the three girls had arrived at the Hamptons, George had met Gary Powell, a test pilot for Jetstream Aviation, a commercial jet manufacturer several miles outside of their town. Someone had stolen the plans for a top secret plane called the Jetstar and sold them to a French company. Nancy had gotten involved because Jetstream suspected Gary of being the thief. At one point in her investigation, Nancy had actually been suspicious of Sasha, but then the mystery took another turn. Sasha was kidnapped by the real villain, and Nancy had had to rescue the Russian dancer.

Nancy studied Sasha's profile. He was charming, impulsive, and romantic. He had a way of making whoever he was with feel special. And he also had presence—when he walked into a room everyone stared.

Yes, Sasha was definitely glamorous. Tommy wasn't, but he was funny and smart and nice. He reminded Nancy a little of her boyfriend, Ned Nickerson.

A fine spray of salt water whipped Nancy's reddish blond hair into her face. She pulled it back idly. It had been a month of excitement, she thought, and for her friends, it was shaping up to be a summer of romance. George and Gary barely spent a minute apart, and now it seemed Bess was falling for Tommy Gray. Nancy couldn't remember the last time her two best friends had been in love at the same time.

Just as she couldn't remember the last time she'd had a real conversation with Ned. Oh, sure, they talked on the phone a couple of times a week, but lately Nancy felt out of touch with him. His summer job in Mapleton was keeping him so busy that he'd had to postpone one trip to visit her already. She missed him, but she was also busy—too busy to think about him as often as she used to, she realized with a pang of guilt.

Tommy threw the powerboat into a sharp curve and Bess gave an admiring sigh. "He drives this thing so well," she cooed.

Nancy pulled herself out of her daydreaming. "Tommy is a great guy," she assured Bess. "And since he manages the waterskiing shop in town, he's *perfect* for you," she added mischievously.

"Perfect for George, you mean," Bess said wryly, referring to her athletic cousin. "Don't think I don't know how silly this seems."

Tommy turned to the girls. "Who's up?" he asked pleasantly. "Bess, do you want to go first?"

"Uh, sure," she said, casting a nervous smile at Nancy. "How hard can it be?" she whispered.

Nancy grinned. "Remember, you've done this before. You'll do fine."

Tommy cut the engine and threw the rope over the back of the boat. "Don't worry, Bess," he said, noticing her reservations. "We picked a good, calm day for it. You have to try it sometime when the wind is really blowing."

As Tommy gave Bess instructions, Sasha came over and sat next to Nancy.

"It is the day for waterskiing amateurs," he said, his deep blue eyes dancing. "Who do you think will be worse at this? Bess or me?"

"Are you kidding? I don't think Bess has willingly participated in a sport in her life!"

The two of them watched as Bess dove over the side and swam to the skis.

"That's it," Tommy said encouragingly as she slipped her feet into the foot holders. "Point the ski tips up out of the water and sit back on the skis with your knees bent."

Bess looked nervous but followed his directions gamely as Tommy eased the boat forward, slowly pulling her out of the water.

"Nancy, do you mind steering while I keep an eye on her?" Tommy asked.

Nodding, Nancy took the wheel, and the three friends watched Bess carefully. She seemed pretty much at ease, Nancy thought with relief. Beside her, Sasha leaned back and shut his eyes.

"Bess tells me you're a detective," Tommy said, standing behind Nancy.

"That's right," she replied, twisting her head to look at him.

"Do you mind talking about work while we're out here?" he asked. "I mean, I don't want to bother you about your job if you'd rather not discuss it."

"Not at all," Nancy assured him. "I'm between mysteries right now, though."

Tommy nodded, but didn't continue.

"Did you want to hear about any of the cases I've solved?" Nancy prodded after a few moments of silence. "Or did you have something to tell me about?"

"Well, actually, it's something new," Tommy admitted, flushing. He broke off. "Bess!" he called, waving to get her attention. "Do it this way!" He crouched, directing Bess to do the same. "She's doing pretty well," he said with admiration.

"I hope you'll be that attentive to me when I get out there," Sasha said to Tommy.

"Are you kidding?" Tommy retorted. "You're an athlete. You won't need it."

"We'll see," Sasha said. "What are you two talking about? I wasn't really listening."

"A mystery," Nancy offered.

"Another one so soon?" Sasha's eyes lit up. "Can I get kidnapped again?"

Seeing his excitement, Nancy suppressed a laugh. Sasha was a mystery buff. It was his enthusiasm for mysteries that had gotten him in trouble the last time.

"Kidnapped?" Tommy frowned, glancing from Nancy to Sasha. "No, I mean, this isn't a big deal," he said, confused. "It's just something that has been worrying my mother. Have you ever heard of Nicholas Scott?"

"The guy who was killed in the boating accident last week?" Nancy asked, surprised. Tommy nodded. "What happened exactly?"

"He was fishing off the end of the island. And his boat hit some rocks."

"Fishing?" Sasha broke in. "I read about that. But I thought it happened at night."

Tommy nodded, one eye on Bess as he spoke. "Night fishing. It's not unusual. But I guess the weather was bad. The wind around here can be violent, especially when it changes direction. Boats get overturned all the time. When Nicholas's boat hit, he was knocked out and drowned."

Not a good swimmer then, Nancy thought. "So you think there's something fishy about the story?"

"Oh, no." Tommy shook his head, simultaneously waving at Bess. "That's not it at all. The problem is that no one has seen his uncle since the accident."

Seeing the blank expression on Nancy's face, Tommy apologized. "Let me start at the beginning. My mother runs the Nisus Art Gallery in town. She has an exclusive arrangement with one of the Hamptons' most prominent painters, Christopher Scott."

Nancy nodded. "I've heard of him. He paints enormous landscapes."

"Right. Nicholas Scott is his nephew, and his agent. *Was,* I guess I should say. They lived together, and Nicholas took care of business so Christopher could concentrate on his work. They were a pretty weird pair.

"Anyway," he continued, "now that Nicholas is gone, Christopher seems to have vanished. Or at least, he's been avoiding everyone. No one answers the telephone at the house or the studio. And the really odd thing is that Christopher didn't even go to Nicholas's funeral."

Nancy frowned. "That *is* strange. Especially if they were close. Maybe he's traveling and doesn't know what happened."

"Maybe." Tommy shrugged doubtfully. "Mom's worried, though. She's got a major show of Scott paintings coming up, and she really needs to speak to him. I don't suppose you could help?"

"Well, I could try," Nancy said slowly. Privately, she thought it didn't seem like much of a mystery, but she would be happy to help. "Has your mother spoken to the police about Scott's disappearance?"

"Oh, no," Tommy said. "See, the thing is, Christopher Scott is a recluse. Everyone knows it. There's no real cause to launch a full-scale investigation—yet."

"What about his friends or relatives?" Sasha asked. "Are they worried, too?"

"There aren't any relatives, at least none that anyone here knows about. As for friends, Christopher wasn't interested in friends. And Nicholas was *not* the world's most popular guy."

"No?" Nancy asked, intrigued.

Tommy frowned. "He was kind of a playboy. He didn't have a job, unless you count taking care of Chris's money as a job. He spent some of his time acting with the local theater group and writing poetry. Mostly, he went to nightclubs and lived off his uncle's money."

"Who arranged for the funeral?" Sasha asked.

"That was also strange," Tommy said. "I think Bob Tercero did. He's the manager at my mom's gallery."

"Well, I could stop by the gallery later today to talk to your mom, if you'd like," Nancy offered.

"*We* could," Sasha interrupted. "I'm free all day."

Tommy grinned. "I'd really appreciate it."

The three young people settled on a time, and Tommy took over the wheel. "Bess looks okay. Why don't you go sit down," he offered.

Nancy and Sasha went to the bow, where Sasha had spread a towel over the deck. Nancy sat on the towel, and Sasha perched, half seated, on the railing.

"You *are* going to let me help with this case?" Sasha asked as he held his lean, high-cheekboned face up toward the sun. He added, "You know we make a good team—in more than one way."

What was she going to do about him? Nancy wondered, as she let her eyes run over his thick, light brown hair. He had made it clear that he was interested in her, and he wasn't going to give up easily. She *did* like being with him, she had to admit, but she was in love with Ned!

"Yes," she said at last. "You'll poke around, anyway, so I might as well include you."

Sasha's eyes popped open, and he gave Nancy a wide grin. "It doesn't sound very exciting," he commented, "but it ought to be easy and safe, not like the last mystery we solved!"

Suddenly there was an earsplitting scream. Startled, Tommy whipped around, his hands still on the steering wheel. The boat swerved, and Nancy was thrown back against the side of the boat.

Sasha was caught off balance. He tried to hold onto the railing, but his hands slipped. Before Nancy could react, Sasha was thrown out of the boat and was somersaulting backward into the water!

Chapter

Two

Tⲟⲙⲙʏ!" Nancy cried out.

Tommy turned to see what had happened and threw the throttle into neutral. "Bess? Sasha? Is everyone okay?"

Nancy leaned over the side of the boat. "Sasha," she called, "are you okay?"

Sasha was treading water. "Just shaken, I think. What happened? Who screamed?"

"I think it was Bess," Nancy said, shading her eyes as she searched for her friend. Bess, in the distance, waved an arm, signaling that she wasn't hurt.

"There she is." Nancy pointed. "We'd better go get her."

Nancy turned back to Sasha, who was swimming gingerly toward the boat. "What's wrong with your arm?" she asked worriedly, noticing that he was favoring his left arm. "Are you okay?"

"I'm fine," Sasha insisted breathlessly. "Throw me a life preserver and go see if Bess is okay."

"She's managing," Nancy said. "Let's get you up first."

Tommy swung the boat around.

"Come up over the side, and stay away from the engines," Nancy directed as Sasha approached the boat.

Together, Nancy and Tommy hauled Sasha back in over the side gunwale. Nancy took a look at his shoulder as Tommy gunned the engine and took off for Bess.

Bess was treading water exactly where she had fallen. She hadn't even tried to swim for the boat.

"Are you okay?" Nancy called as they drew up beside her. Bess nodded.

Tommy helped Bess aboard, and Nancy dove into the water to retrieve the skis. When she got back Bess was wrapped in a towel, leaning heavily against Tommy's shoulder.

"I'm sorry!" Bess burst out as Nancy hoisted herself back on board. "I didn't mean to fall and cause such a commotion. Sasha, are you sure you're okay?"

Sasha assured her for the third time that he was. "I shouldn't have been sitting on the railing anyway," he said.

13

"What happened to you?" Nancy asked Bess.

"She fell," Tommy said simply. "Happens to the best of us." Turning back to Bess, he brushed damp tendrils of hair off her forehead. "You are okay, aren't you?" he asked tenderly.

Nancy smiled openly as she watched them. The romance was certainly blooming! "Okay if I take the wheel?" she asked.

Tommy nodded, barely glancing at her.

Nancy looked at Sasha. "Uh," she began, "Sasha, do you want to ski?"

"Go ahead, Sasha," Bess said immediately. "Don't let me spoil the day."

Sasha shook his head, salt water flying from his golden brown hair. "That's okay, I've been in the water enough for today." He touched his left shoulder unconsciously.

"You're sure your shoulder is okay?" Nancy asked him worriedly. "Dmitri will kill me if you're hurt."

Sasha grinned at the thought of his overprotective chaperon, Dmitri Kolchak. "He won't kill you, but he will fuss over me more than Tommy is fussing over Bess."

"Let's spend the rest of the day on land," he said, and Nancy headed toward the dock.

"I did *not* fall on purpose!" Bess declared hotly as the two girls and Sasha sat on the porch of the Nisus Art Gallery after a very late lunch.

Nancy laughed and hugged her friend. "Bess,

I'm teasing! All I meant was it couldn't have worked better if you had planned it."

A small smile played over Bess's lips. "Well, Tommy *was* awfully concerned—" She stopped suddenly, narrowing her eyes. "Don't you dare tell George I fell! She'll never let me forget it."

Tommy poked his head out the door. "Are you guys coming in?" he called.

The three friends walked into the gallery, cool air embracing them. The main room was a large, off-white space, sparsely furnished. There was a young woman sitting at a desk near the door, reading a book. Nancy looked around.

An enormous painting hung on the wall facing them, dominating the room. It was done entirely in shades of pink, and it was very pretty, but Nancy didn't think it was special. "I'd never make an art critic," she murmured to Sasha.

A smattering of smaller paintings graced the other walls. Two sculptures were displayed on freestanding columns placed in the middle of the room.

Tommy motioned them over to where he was standing with a tall, elegant woman.

"Nancy Drew, Sasha Petrov, this is my mother, Cynthia Gray," Tommy said. "And you've met Bess."

Nancy shook hands with the handsome older woman, who was dressed in layers of flowing peach silk. "Nice to meet you."

"And you," Cynthia responded warmly. "I'm

glad you could come," she said, refocusing her attention to include Sasha.

"We want to help in any way we can," Sasha offered.

"Well, then, why don't we go into my office?" Cynthia invited, leading them across the room. "I'm afraid I won't be much help, but I'll tell you everything I know."

"Um, Nancy," Bess called. "Do you need me? Tommy wants to show me some of Christopher Scott's work."

"Good idea," Nancy said, as she and Sasha followed Cynthia down a hall and into a quiet and perfectly decorated office. Cynthia had hung a few paintings on the taupe fabric-covered walls. A small bronze statue was spotlighted next to the door. "Your gallery is beautiful," Nancy said sincerely.

"Thank you." Cynthia shrugged. "It's really just a hobby for me, but I have fun with it. Now, what can I tell you? Tommy says you're willing to help me."

"Well," Nancy began, "Tommy said you were worried about Christopher Scott, and we'd like to know why specifically."

Cynthia nodded. "I am. He's absolutely disappeared. I have a major show of his work coming up in a few days and I *have* to have him here!"

"You've tried contacting any family members?" Sasha asked.

"Bob has. Bob Tercero is my manager. He works out all the details around here."

"He's the one who arranged Nicholas's funeral?" Nancy asked.

Cynthia nodded. "Chris didn't even show up for that." She stopped suddenly. "Maybe you could go to Chris's studio to check it out for clues. Bob went by there, but maybe a detective could find something that he missed."

"I'll go," Nancy agreed, "but first I should probably get some more information about Christopher. Did he say anything about going on a trip?"

"Oh, goodness, I have no idea!" Cynthia said, surprised. "You know, I can't remember the last time I spoke to him.

"I'm sorry, you must think I'm crazy," Cynthia continued sheepishly. "Bob really runs the show around here. I just stop in and put the finishing touches on things. Most of my dealings with Chris were worked out between Nicholas and Bob." She wrinkled her nose. "Nicholas Scott was not the most pleasant person to deal with. Bob was a friend of his. It was a lot easier to let the two of them take care of business."

"Is Bob around?" Sasha asked.

Cynthia picked up the phone. "Bob? Could you come to my office, please?"

While they waited, Cynthia said, "We'll help you any way we can. It's just me, Bob, and our receptionist, Cecilia. I'll tell her to cooperate with you, too. She's a college student and just works summers. I'll introduce you on the way out."

A few minutes later a broad, dark-skinned man

with black eyes and hair breezed into the room. Cynthia introduced him to Nancy and Sasha and excused herself.

"I'm glad you're here to help," Bob Tercero said, settling himself behind Cynthia's desk. "I'm worried sick about Christopher."

"I know this may seem silly," Nancy began carefully, "but I'm afraid I'm a little confused. You're worried sick, and Cynthia is, too, but still no one seems to think this is serious enough to take to the police."

"Well, Christopher is famous for dropping out of sight. Most of the townies just assume he's out of the country."

"And?"

"And . . . I don't know," Bob said, exhaling slowly. "It seems like the only reasonable explanation, but I talked to Nicholas the day he died, and he told me Chris was working furiously."

"Cynthia tells me you and Nicholas were friends," Nancy said.

Bob nodded. "Good friends. We did quite a lot together."

Nancy glanced over at Sasha. Bob didn't seem to be in mourning for his "good friend."

"Well, then, perhaps you can tell us how to get to the Scotts' house?"

"I can do better than that," Bob said eagerly. "I'll take you there."

Nancy shook her head. "No, thanks. It's nice of you to offer, but the fewer people, the easier any investigation is."

Bob's smile faded.

"Please don't take it as an insult," Nancy said. "It's just the way I work."

"I thought I could help you," Bob said stiffly. "It's not as though Nicholas had many friends. In fact, toward the end, I may have been his only one. He wasn't a very nice person, you know."

"But he was a good friend of yours?" Sasha asked doubtfully.

"Well, we had a working relationship. Christopher is the gallery's most important client, so I devoted a lot of my time to working with the Scotts."

"You said he wasn't a nice person," Nancy prompted. "What exactly did you mean?"

"I mean he was nasty. He was arrogant. He had a violent temper, and he treated people terribly."

Bob placed his arms on the desk and leaned across them. "In fact, Nicholas had so many enemies, I wouldn't be the least bit surprised if someone had decided to get rid of him for good!"

Chapter

Three

ARE YOU SAYING someone murdered Nicholas Scott?" Nancy asked.

"Uh, no, not really," Bob said, suddenly defensive. "I only meant that there are people around who hated him enough to kill him."

Nancy studied Bob more carefully. He was acting very oddly. First he said Nicholas was a friend, then he changed his mind and told them Nicholas was a business associate and that he was nasty and selfish. *Then* he came out with the statement that Nicholas could have been murdered and then quickly reversed himself, saying it was an accident. It seemed as if Bob was trying to slander his friend without actually doing it. Nancy wasn't sure why, especially since Nicholas's character wasn't the issue. It couldn't have anything to do with Christopher's disappearance.

"So there was nothing strange about his death?" she asked.

"No. The police looked into it very carefully," Bob replied. "The investigation is closed. It was an accident."

Nancy decided not to question Bob further, and she and Sasha stood up to go. Bob escorted them back down the hall. "This is one of Scott's recent paintings," he said, gesturing toward the huge pink canvas hanging in the main room.

As Nancy and Sasha stood studying the painting again, Bob asked suddenly, "I wonder if you could do me a favor when you check out the Scott place? One of Christopher's paintings is missing.

"It's called *Vanity*," Bob continued. "It's an oil that Chris did about six months ago of a woman sitting in front of a mirror, combing her hair. You can't miss it; she's a pretty girl with long red hair. It's a very striking image."

"How do you know it's missing?" Sasha asked.

"It belongs to the gallery. We bought it, but Christopher had a hard time parting with it, so we let him keep it for a while. I was at the house when I was making arrangements for the funeral, and I noticed it wasn't in its usual place."

Nancy looked skeptical. "Isn't it odd for a painter to sell something but keep it in his house?"

"Well, I think he was doing another portrait, or

maybe a whole series, and he needed the *Vanity* for reference," Bob replied. "Christopher is a little odd, you know. A genius, but a little odd."

"Was there anything unusual about the painting?" Nancy asked. "Any reason why it would be missing?"

Bob shook his head. "Nothing unusual. Well," he corrected himself, "Christopher doesn't usually paint portraits. He's really a landscape painter, but I don't think that could be a reason for the painting to be missing."

"What about the model?" Nancy asked. "Could he have given it to her?"

"Nah." Bob dismissed the idea. "Besides, we paid for it."

"Maybe we should check with her anyway," Sasha ventured.

"Good luck!" Bob replied. "People here come and go all the time. I don't have a clue how you'd even begin to look for her."

"She doesn't live around here?" Nancy asked.

"No, she was just someone who was here briefly. I don't even know what her name is."

Nancy nodded. "Thank you for your time," she said.

"No problem. Thank *you* for helping us look for Christopher. If we don't find him, it's going to be a problem for the gallery."

Nancy and Sasha found Bess and Tommy outside. After Tommy offered to lead the way to the Scotts' place, Nancy signaled Bess that she wanted to talk to her. The girls jumped into Nancy's car, and Sasha reluctantly joined Tommy in his jeep. They drove through the center of the bustling beach town on its wide main street, which was lined with boutiques and quaint shops.

After Nancy told Bess about her conversations with Bob and Cynthia, Bess said, "Wait. Is this mystery about Christopher or his nephew?"

"I'm not sure," Nancy admitted. "I'll have to check out Nicholas's death just to be sure. This mystery may be more interesting than I thought."

The girls followed Tommy out of town and into the residential area. They passed huge old-fashioned houses set back on perfectly manicured lawns edged with masses of summer flowers in every color.

"This is such a beautiful little town," Bess said as they went along. The road was shaded by a canopy of large trees that looked as though they'd been there forever.

"It smells so clean, just a hint of the sea in the air," Nancy added.

As they drove the houses thinned out and were set even farther back from the road. Soon massive hedges blocked the girls' view of the properties completely.

Following Tommy, Nancy turned her silver Honda into a long, private driveway. No house was visible from the road.

23

"Look at this place!" Bess gasped as she watched a sprawling wooden house rise from the sloping, grassy yard. It had a gray gabled roof and a deck that wrapped around the second story. "It's a mansion!"

The two cars pulled up in front of the house.

"Just how do we get in?" Sasha asked, slamming his door. "I thought the whole point was that no one's home."

"That's easy," Tommy said, pushing back a branch of one of the blue hydrangeas that lined each side of the front walk. He stooped and came up with a key. "Nicholas always kept his key hidden here under the front step."

They split into two groups to search the house. The guys checked out the downstairs, and Nancy and Bess took the second floor. They started in the master bedroom, Christopher's room.

"Do you think Christopher could have killed Nicholas and skipped town?" Bess asked, kneeling to peer under the queen-size bed.

"Possibly," Nancy replied. "But if he did, it doesn't look like he took anything with him." Nancy showed Bess the bathroom, where the sink was covered with toiletries. "He would have left in an awful hurry."

Bess returned to the bedroom and opened the closet door. "You're right. This closet is stuffed. If he has more clothes than these, I don't know where he would have put them. What are we looking for?"

"I don't know," Nancy said. She swung the

door to the bedroom open and checked behind it. "Anything unusual."

The girls walked down the hall to search the next room.

"This must have been Nicholas's bedroom," Bess commented in a low voice.

"It doesn't look as if anyone has cleaned it since the accident," Nancy commented.

The girls searched the smaller bedroom quickly, sifting through the clothes draped over the back of an overstuffed chair in one corner and checking the drawers and surfaces.

"Just the usual stuff," Nancy said when they had finished.

After the girls searched the guest rooms, they headed back downstairs to meet Sasha and Tommy in the entrance hall.

"Nothing," Tommy reported. "Everything looks normal."

"And no portrait of the red-haired girl," Sasha added. "I checked everywhere."

"It's strange," Nancy mused as they left the house. "Only two paintings in the whole place. And nothing to indicate a painter lives or works here. No oils, canvases, nothing."

"They'd be in his studio," Tommy said. "It's a separate building."

Nancy snapped her fingers. "Of course. I should have known. Can we go there and investigate now?"

"It's six o'clock," Bess said. "What about tonight?"

"Oh, that's right." Nancy glanced at her watch. "We're going out tonight. But this shouldn't take much longer here."

"Nancy," Bess protested, "I promised George we'd be back by six. We're late already. Besides, I still have to decide what I'm going to wear tonight."

"The studio's just over that way," Tommy said, pointing. "Why don't I take Bess back to your aunt's and you two can check out the studio?"

"Great idea!" Nancy said. "Bess can pick out something for me to wear, too," she added mischievously.

"Oh, no! I'll never have time to choose *two* outfits!" Bess wailed.

Nancy and Sasha set out across the back lawn in the direction Tommy had pointed. As the ocean came into view, they saw a small, square outbuilding. It was an old, two-story structure facing the water. A short, clipped hedge ran along the far side of it, defining the end of the Scott property. A fragile-looking wooden dock reached out into the bay right below the house. Several powerboats and a sailboat were moored along one side of it, swinging gently in the surge.

"That's got to be the studio," Nancy said, shading her eyes from the slanting sun bouncing off the water. They veered off toward the building. As they approached, Nancy noticed a light on in one of the rooms.

"Sasha," she asked, putting her hand on his arm, "do you see what I see?"

Sasha looked at her, then back at the small building. Just as he did, a shadow passed across a window.

"Well, what do you know?" he said under his breath. "Someone's inside!"

Chapter

Four

D₀ ᴠᴏᴜ ᴛʜɪɴᴋ it's Christopher?" Sasha asked.

"Only one way to find out," Nancy replied. They walked around to the front, to where a door had been cut into the wide opening of the original building. The building must have been a boat house before its conversion to a studio, Nancy decided. The first floor had large plate-glass windows overlooking the water.

Nancy knocked on the door and waited.

When the door finally swung open, a petite girl was standing beside it, her hand on the knob. Her dark brown hair hung in shoulder-length ringlets, and her soft brown eyes looked sad.

"I'm sorry to disturb you," Nancy said. "We're looking for Christopher Scott."

"He's not here," the girl replied. Her eyes instantly filled with tears. "No one's here."

"Do you mind if we come in?" Nancy asked.

The girl released the doorknob and walked into the living room. Nancy glanced at Sasha and they followed, closing the door behind them.

The living room took up almost all of the ground floor. It was shabby, furnished with a rickety rattan couch and a few unmatched armchairs. The flowered cushions on the couch were faded, and the coarse outdoor carpet that covered most of the floor hadn't been cleaned in a while.

"I'm Megan Archer," the girl said as she sat down and motioned for them to join her. "Are you friends of Christopher's?"

"Actually, no," Nancy said. She and Sasha introduced themselves. "Cynthia Gray asked us to come by. She's worried about Christopher."

Megan nodded mechanically, tucking her slender legs under her on the couch. She smoothed her brightly printed skirt over her knees and looked down. After an uncomfortable pause, Nancy asked, "And you?"

"I'm . . . I was Nicholas's girlfriend," Megan said. She put her hand to her forehead and laughed, a hint of desperation in her voice. "We were together for four months. That's all. It's kind of silly to be so upset after only four months, don't you think?"

"No," Nancy said quietly, leaning in toward the girl. "I'm sorry for your loss."

29

Megan lifted her delicate face and fixed her eyes on Nancy. "You must think it's strange, finding me here. I live right across the hedge, so it's very convenient. I used to spend a lot of time here."

"So you know Christopher, then," Sasha stated, sitting on a chair opposite the girl. "Do you know where he is now?"

"No, I'm afraid I don't. In fact, I've never seen him. He's not around much."

"I understand he's a recluse," Nancy said, probing delicately.

Megan shrugged. "I don't know. I do know he travels a lot. Nicholas always said Christopher just didn't have any patience with people."

"Do you mean you never met him once?" Sasha asked. "Not even in his own studio?"

Megan looked at him in surprise. "Well, no. But I'm not here every minute. I work during the day, and I guess Christopher also does most of his work during the day. There are new paintings lying around sometimes."

"Is there a painting here that he's working on now?" Nancy asked.

"If he is, I haven't seen it. The studio's upstairs," Megan said, pointing to a spiral staircase near the door. "There's nothing up there now, though."

Nancy changed the subject. "Tell me about Nicholas," she suggested.

As Megan spoke, Nancy did her best to hide her surprise. The girl's description was obviously colored by love—it was the exact opposite of Bob Tercero's. And of Tommy's and Cynthia's, too, she realized. According to Megan, Nicholas spent all his time taking care of his uncle. He was a sensitive, artistic person who adored Megan so much that they spent most of their evenings alone together at the studio, rarely seeing anyone.

When Megan finished, Nancy asked her about the *Vanity* painting.

"Vanity?" Megan asked. "I can't think of anything by that name."

But as Nancy described the painting, Megan's face changed.

"Absolutely not," she declared. "There is no such painting. I'm sure I would have seen it if there was."

Nancy glanced at Sasha, her eyes warning him to be quiet. Megan was being awfully decisive, she thought. Especially since she had been so vague about everything else. She made a mental note to pursue this later.

"Do you mind if we look around?" Nancy asked mildly, standing up.

"Not at all," Megan said. She stood up. "I have to leave anyway, so please close the door behind you as you go. Don't worry about locking up—as you can see, there's nothing worth stealing here."

Megan was right. Other than the few pieces of furniture, the place was eerily empty. There was a kitchenette at the back of the main floor, which looked as if it hadn't been used in years.

Nancy and Sasha went upstairs to look at the

studio. The room was almost bare. A large easel stood in one corner, surrounded by a ring of paint splatters.

Leaning against one wall were several blank canvases of different sizes. Other than that, there was nothing to indicate that this was the studio of a working artist, Nancy realized. And no sign of the *Vanity* painting.

"Well," Sasha said, when they completed their search, "this wasn't very helpful."

"When you're a detective, you need to see the things that aren't there as well as the ones that are," Nancy replied, as they left the house. "Sometimes the clue is that there's nothing unusual to be found."

"Are you saying that you did find a clue?" Sasha asked in delight.

"No." Nancy shook her head. "Not this time. But did you notice how different Megan's description of Nicholas was from Bob Tercero's?"

"That's nothing," Sasha said, crinkling his nose dismissively. "That's just love talking." Then he gave Nancy a sideways glance. "Love makes you do the strangest things," he added softly.

Nancy ignored that. She had enough to think about right then!

She and Sasha headed back to town. She dropped him off at his house and wearily made her way back to Eloise Drew's house. It was a large, contemporary beach house set back a short distance from the beach. Nancy walked through the front door and sifted through the pile of mail on the table in the entrance hall.

"Anybody home?" she called. She looked around the airy living room, which took up most of the main floor.

Getting no response, Nancy climbed the stairs to the room that she was sharing with Bess and George. Music was booming out of their half-open door. No wonder no one had heard her!

"Hey, Nancy!" Bess called gaily, throwing a red blouse onto a pile of clothes on her bed. "We thought you'd never get here."

"But don't worry," George Fayne said laconically from a chair in the corner, "you haven't missed anything. She *still* hasn't found the perfect thing to wear."

The big room was a mess. The girls rotated between the two twin beds and a futon on the floor. With all the furniture, it was hard to keep it neat in the first place, but when Bess was getting ready to go out it always looked as if a storm had just torn through it.

Nancy saw several of her own blouses and dresses among the pile of things Bess had rejected. Shaking her head in amusement, she set her purse down among the clothes strewn on one bed and greeted George.

George and Bess were total opposites. George was tall and athletic, and wore her dark hair stylishly short. She was cool in a crisis and always had practical advice. George teased Bess constantly about her passion for clothes and her endless string of crushes, but despite their differences the two cousins were fiercely loyal and devoted to each other.

"Where's Aunt Eloise?" Nancy asked.

"Out with Dana Harding, I think," George answered, referring to the director of the dance institute. Nancy's aunt had become friendly with several of the women in the area. "The way Eloise fits into this town, you'd think she grew up here."

"You'd better start getting ready, Nancy," Bess advised, examining what looked like her twentieth outfit in a full-length mirror. "I was just telling George about my day. Tommy told me all about the gallery on the way home. Do you know how much a painting goes for these days?" She didn't wait for an answer. "There's not a single painting in his mom's gallery under twenty thousand dollars! And the gallery is just Cynthia's hobby!"

"They sound rich," George commented. "Just what you always wanted—a rich boyfriend."

"I guess they are pretty well-off. Tell Nancy about your day."

"Yeah. What were you and Gary up to?" Nancy asked.

George shrugged. "He worked this morning. Then he took me flying. What about you, Nan?" she asked as Nancy selected a deep green dress from Bess's discard pile. "How's Sasha?"

Nancy blushed. "Okay, I guess."

"Okay!" Bess snorted. "You should see the two of them. Sparks positively fly when they're together. What a hunk!"

"Bess," Nancy said, feeling slightly irritated. "He's just a friend."

"Well, every girl in the Hamptons is jealous of the way your 'friend' follows you around," Bess countered. "The minute we go anywhere, girls swarm all over him."

"I'm going to take a shower," Nancy announced. "If you two boy-crazy girls want to talk about me, do it while I'm gone."

But the truth was Nancy couldn't get Sasha off her mind. She knew she couldn't put him off much longer—the things he had said that day were proof that he was getting tired of being "just friends."

But what did *she* want? Sasha was fun and exciting, and—well, *different* from any other guy she'd ever met. She could definitely be interested in him—except for Ned.

Oh, Ned. Nancy sighed, toweling herself off. She did still love him, but Sasha was certainly putting that love to the test. The dancer was like a whirlwind, so intense and charming, and so interested in her.

Nancy slipped the dress on and rubbed a dry circle on the steamy mirror to see herself. Made of thin, silky cotton and cut straight, the dress showed off her slender figure to perfection. Sasha would just love it, she thought, and then stopped short as she realized where her mind had wandered. "Oh, no!" she groaned. She had to make a decision soon.

"This place is great!" Bess exclaimed as the three girls and their escorts stepped into the Lobster Tank, one of the most popular clubs in town. It was a large, dimly lit room, pulsing with rock music. George began tapping her foot.

"Care to dance?" Gary asked George.

Nancy watched as George and Gary stepped onto the dance floor. Gary's lean body shifted back and forth gracefully to the beat, and he smiled down at George as he took her hand. George gazed back at him and grinned. They were perfect for each other, Nancy decided, sitting at a table with Sasha.

The song ended, and a slower one with a strong Latin beat came on. Nancy found herself being pulled out of her chair by Sasha.

"Last time we went dancing, I left you alone," he said in her ear as he guided her out onto the floor. "This time we must dance."

Nancy closed her eyes, swaying her slim hips gently to the beat. When she opened them again, Sasha's intense blue gaze was fixed on her face, the glittering light playing over his golden brown hair. Her heart pounded. He was so handsome!

Sasha twirled Nancy around and pulled her close. They came face-to-face, and for a breathless moment she thought he was going to kiss her. The moment passed, and Nancy fought down the feeling of disappointment that swept through her.

"You have been promising to come by and take a dance lesson with me for ages now," Sasha shouted over the music. "What about tomorrow?"

Nancy hesitated.

"Being with me is not so bad, is it?" he asked, pretending to be hurt.

Nancy's determination faded, and she laughed. A dance lesson wasn't a date, after all. And how could she resist? "Of course not," she said, touching his cheek. "Tomorrow's fine."

Maybe she didn't have to make a big decision right now, she thought. He wasn't pushing her, and she was having a great time. They were just friends still, after all. Maybe she should just wait and see what happened.

After a couple of hours at the club, Nancy and her friends decided to head home. Laughing, they burst into the parking lot, Nancy and Sasha first. Bess realized she'd left her brush in the powder room and dashed back in, pulling George along for company.

"We'll wait out here," Nancy said, declining the invitation to join them.

"So will we," Gary said as he and Tommy stopped just outside the main door.

It had been hot in the club. Nancy and Sasha moved over to her car and leaned back against it. The cool night breeze blew Nancy's damp hair away from her face. She shivered.

"Cold?" Sasha asked, slipping his arm around her.

"No," Nancy murmured, pulling away reluctantly. "The breeze feels nice."

"Nan!" Bess called as the cousins appeared in the doorway of the club. She broke away from George and the guys and jogged up to the two of them. "I saw that arm," she whispered playfully in Nancy's ear. "Just friends?"

"Bess, really—" Nancy began.

Bess held up her hands in mock surrender. "That's not why I interrupted. Here." She handed Nancy an envelope. "It's for you."

Nancy took it in her hand. It was a plain white envelope with her name typed neatly in the center. "What's this?" she asked, turning it over.

"Beats me," Bess shrugged. "Danny, the bouncer, said someone left it on the counter of the coatroom."

Sasha looked at Nancy, surprised. "Who knew you were here?"

"No one I can think of, besides my aunt Eloise," Nancy said. "My car was parked right here, and Tommy's jeep is easy enough to recognize."

Nancy slit the envelope open before Sasha could protest. "Don't worry," she said, pulling a sheet of paper out. "It's not a bomb."

Nancy unfolded the paper. It wasn't a bomb, but the three words typed there took her breath away. The note read: Scott was murdered!

Chapter

Five

NICHOLAS SCOTT MURDERED? Nancy's mind raced. What did this mean? And who could have left her the message? Bob Tercero had mentioned murder. Could he have been afraid to say something more? Or had someone else she didn't even know left it?

While the others waited in the parking lot, Nancy and Sasha went back into the Lobster Tank to question the bouncer, Danny, who had given Bess the note.

Danny scratched his head. "I don't know why anyone would leave a note at the coat check. It's never open in summer, so there's no one on duty there. If I hadn't seen the envelope and recognized your name, chances are we never would have known it was there. Someone would have found it at the end of the night and thrown it away, probably."

Telling Nancy and Sasha to wait, Danny checked with a few other members of the staff, but no one had seen the person who left the note.

"Well, that was useless," Nancy grumbled as she and Sasha headed back outside. They told the others what they had—or rather, hadn't—learned. No one was able to come up with any suggestions for how to find the note writer. Finally they all headed for home.

The next morning Nancy woke up early. After a quick breakfast she jumped into her car and drove out to Megan Archer's place, hoping to catch the girl before she left for work. This was the second time someone had suggested Nicholas Scott was murdered, and Nancy was determined to find out why.

Remembering that Megan had said she lived on the other side of the hedge from the Scotts, Nancy found her house easily. It was a small cottage at the end of a rough gravel road—judging from the fancy neighborhood, it was probably someone's guest house.

Megan seemed pleased to see Nancy and invited her into the living room.

"I was just having coffee before I go to work," she said, leading Nancy to a round breakfast table in front of a picture window. The window gave Nancy a beautiful view of the bay. "Please have some. It's nice to have someone to talk to."

Nancy poured herself a cup of coffee, put cream in, and stirred the mixture. "Do you have time to talk to me?" she asked. Megan nodded. "I need your help," Nancy said simply.

Megan looked at her with a steady, level gaze, inviting her to continue.

"I heard that Nicholas was murdered," Nancy continued.

"Murdered?" Megan asked, horrified. She stood up and stared out the window, hugging herself with her arms. Nancy could see tears forming in her dark eyes. "I don't know where you heard *that,* but it's ridiculous."

"You're sure?" Nancy pressed. "Someone is trying very hard to make me think it was no accident."

"Of course I'm sure," Megan said, impatiently running her hands through her glossy curls. "I was with him right before—before it happened.

"It was late at night," she continued, staring out at the bay. "The weather was terrible. The wind and the surge alone would probably have been enough to tip the boat. I'm sure Nicholas wasn't paying attention to what he was doing, and the boat went off course and hit the rocks."

Nancy prodded her. "Why go out at night?"

"He did it all the time. Night fishing is very popular. They catch a lot of striped bass after dark and in the early hours of the morning. Nicholas had also been very moody, and going out in the boat seemed to calm him down."

Megan swung around, her square chin tilted defiantly. "There's another thing. We had a fight. It was silly, but he blew up at me and slammed out the door. If we hadn't fought, he would never have gotten into the boat." Megan sat down again and rested her head in her hands.

Nancy felt awful. Now she understood that Megan thought she was responsible for Nicholas's death.

"So you see," Megan said softly, raising her tearstained face, "all the rumors are wrong."

"What was the fight about?" Nancy asked.

"His moods, his strange behavior. He was worried about money, and about Chris's paintings—although he wouldn't explain why." Megan sighed. "The last couple of weeks he was alive, he walked around with a great weight on him. I wanted him to share his problems with me, but he said he couldn't."

Nancy believed Megan was telling the truth, but she knew there could be more to the story that Megan didn't even know. For example, Nicholas could have deliberately picked a fight with Megan as an excuse to take the boat out. Perhaps he was involved in something he didn't want her to know about—something illegal, maybe.

Nancy frowned, annoyed with herself. This was all just speculation. She needed facts!

"Can you tell me where it happened?" she asked Megan.

Megan smiled bitterly. "I wish I could forget! It happened near Montauk, the town at the end of the island. Do you want to see?"

"It might help," Nancy ventured. "If you have time. Don't you have to get to work?"

"I can go in late today," Megan said, and slipped on a pair of sneakers. She grabbed a pair of low-heeled pumps and her purse and put them in the backseat of Nancy's car.

As Nancy drove Megan out toward Montauk, they chatted about the town. Megan had been in the Hamptons for only four months.

"I hardly qualify as a townie," Megan explained. "It'll be years before that."

"People here have deep roots, don't they?" Nancy commented. "I met a woman who told me she was from one of the 'first families.' They'd been around for generations."

Megan smiled. "Take this turn," she directed. "We can get down to the beach this way."

As the two girls walked along the shore, Megan pointed to some rocks breaking the surface far offshore.

"This whole area is a good fishing spot," Megan explained as they walked. "Nicholas's boat was ripped up on those rocks—it's still there."

"Still there?" Nancy was surprised. "You mean it sank?"

Megan nodded, looking at her curiously.

"It's just that I thought boats had to float to be certified by the coast guard," Nancy explained. "They have all sorts of regulations about having buoyant material in every part of a boat so it can't sink."

"Not old boats," Megan corrected her. "They still use some of the old aluminum and steel dories around here. The boat Nicholas was in when he died was aluminum."

Nancy shaded her eyes. "How deep is the water?"

"It varies. The beaches are shallow, but I think it gets down to about forty-five feet."

Perfect for scuba diving, Nancy thought. And she had a couple of friends who'd love to go.

Nancy dropped Megan off at work, then went back to her aunt's house to call the police station. According to the desk sergeant, the police had sent divers down, but the boat wasn't salvageable, so they had simply left it underwater. She was told that the sergeant in charge of the investigation was away for two days, but she could call back then if she had more questions.

As Nancy hung up, Bess walked into the kitchen.

"There you are," Bess said while looking in the refrigerator. She grabbed a can of soda and popped the top open. "Want to come down to the beach with us?"

"Actually, I had another outing in mind," Nancy said. "Who's 'us,' by the way?"

"George, Gary, and Tommy," Bess said.

Nancy playfully poked her friend in the ribs. "So it's getting serious?"

Bess got a dreamy look in her eyes. "Oh, Nan, Tommy is incredible! He's so down-to-earth—he really listens to me when I talk, you know what I mean? Do you think he likes me?"

"I'm positive he does," Nancy declared. "All you have to do is look at him to see he's got a major crush on you."

"Well, then, I'd better not leave him pining on the beach," she said. "So what's this outing you have in mind? Not more waterskiing, I hope."

"No." Nancy smiled. "Scuba diving."

"Why?"

"I'll tell you all together. Okay?" Nancy asked.

Bess rolled her eyes. "Well, everyone will love it. Except me, of course. I'm not certified."

"You can stay with the boat," Nancy said. "You know you tan best on the water."

Still grumbling, Bess headed down to the beach to get the others. They promised to meet at Pete's Dive Shop.

Nancy called the dance institute to see if Sasha was done rehearsing. He had just finished, and she arranged to pick him up in ten minutes.

She explained scuba diving to Sasha on the way to the dive shop. He wasn't certified to dive, either, so he was going to stay with Bess on the boat. As the others tried on their diving gear and waited for their tanks, Nancy explained what they were doing and what she wanted them to look for.

"I want you to search the area for any clue as to what Nicholas was doing out on his boat in the middle of the night. Maybe he really was fishing. But maybe he was trying to get rid of something or pick something up." She turned to Tommy. "I'd like you to take a look at the engine, if it's still in one piece. Check the steering cable to see if it's been cut. It's a long shot, but we may as well try it."

"Nancy," Tommy began. "You should know that these waters are famous for sharks."

Everyone turned to Tommy in surprise.

"It shouldn't be a problem," he added quickly. "I just wanted everyone to be aware of it. The biggest great white shark ever recorded was hooked in Montauk Bay."

Gary looked at Tommy uneasily. "I don't mean to sound like a coward, but my specialty is the air, not the water. Is it safe or isn't it?"

"It should be. There haven't been any reports of shark attacks for a while. If you *do* see one, don't panic, just stay where you are. It's very important to keep still and not thrash around. If you do, they think you're hurt, and they're more likely to come over and investigate."

"We don't have to go if you don't want to," Nancy offered. "Should we vote? Who wants to risk it?"

Four hands, including Nancy's, shot up immediately. Bess and Sasha didn't vote.

Nancy smiled. "Then here we go," she declared.

Soon the group was on its way with Tommy driving their borrowed boat. Bess stood beside him at the wheel as he steered toward the accident site. Their blond hair was almost the exact same color. Tommy whispered into Bess's ear, and she nodded back at him, her face glowing. Nancy smiled at them from the bow of the boat where she and Sasha were sitting.

Romance was in the air, all right! Bess and Tommy couldn't keep their eyes off each other. George and Gary had been together longer, and the electricity between them had turned into familiarity, each knowing what the other was thinking. George was positively radiant.

As Nancy watched her two best friends, their laughter rising and falling over the drone of the engine, she felt Sasha's arm slip around her waist. A thrill of emotion ran through her, and without thinking she leaned back against his shoulder.

The sun was beating down and Sasha's strong arm was tight around her. Her heart was pounding in her ears. She closed her eyes and let herself relax against him.

When he turned and her cheek touched his sun-warmed skin, she was startled and her eyes flew open. This was too much, she realized suddenly. Things were moving too fast. Before it went any further, she had to be sure she was doing the right thing. She leaned forward, pretending to study something on the water.

"We're here!" Bess said as Tommy cut the

engine right then. Everyone sprang into action. Sasha threw the anchor overboard and paddled the boat back until the hook caught on the bottom and pulled tight. After double-checking their equipment, the four divers fell backward into the ocean.

Treading water, Nancy cleared her mask and put her regulator in her mouth. She gave Tommy the okay sign, and together they dove, a white burst of bubbles trailing behind them after each breath.

Nancy gazed around, getting used to the feeling of wearing scuba equipment again. Most of the diving she'd done had been in tropical oceans, where the water was clear and swarming with colorful fish. But here the water was cloudy, and she didn't see any fish. In fact, she didn't see any living things, other than herself and her friends. It felt creepy.

Once on the bottom, she could just make out a boat off to their right. It was about fifteen feet away, and all she could really see through the murk was the shadowy outline of a hull. She touched Tommy's arm, and the two of them swam toward it. George caught up to Nancy and signaled that Gary had a cramp in his leg. They were going up. Nancy nodded.

As she and Tommy approached the boat, Tommy began shaking his head at Nancy. He pointed to the hull, then waved his hands vigorously.

Nancy looked around uneasily. Was he warning her about sharks? she wondered. Then Tommy reached out and wiped his finger across the bow, leaving a mark in the layer of algae that covered the boat.

Nancy nodded. He was telling her that this wasn't the wreck they were looking for. This one had been underwater too long.

Tommy kicked away from the wreck and hung suspended in the water, trying to determine in which direction the current was pulling them.

They set out with the current. Soon Nancy saw the dim outline of another hull.

This time they had found it. Nancy and Tommy swam slowly around the heavy metal boat. It was twisted into the rocks, making it impossible to pry free without heavy equipment. No wonder the police had left it, Nancy thought.

After a half hour Tommy shrugged. Pointing to the engine, he indicated with an okay sign that it was in good condition and the steering cable seemed fine. The gauge on the gas tank, which was lashed into the boat near the engine, showed it was half full.

As Nancy was probing the gaping hole in the bow where the boat had hit the rocks, Tommy signaled to her that he was swimming away for a minute but that he'd be right back. Nancy watched him disappear into a cave.

Nancy felt frustrated as she continued searching the bottom for any clue to the accident. Gradually she began to feel short of breath. She checked the gauge on her tank. It said she had plenty of air. What was wrong? Was her regulator failing?

Nancy scanned the area. Tommy was nowhere in sight. She estimated the distance to the cave. It was too far to get there easily.

Nancy strained to get a breath, but no air came out of the mouthpiece. She took the regulator out of her mouth and tapped her finger on the valve. She couldn't push it in to release the air. Something was stuck in it. She hit it a couple of times, but it didn't budge.

It was no good. Her regulator was useless, and she was all alone under forty-five feet of water!

Chapter

Six

GET HOLD OF YOURSELF, DREW, Nancy ordered silently. She eyed the surface, wondering if she could make the air in her lungs last. The pressure in her chest was mounting.

Remembering diving procedure, Nancy kicked slowly toward the silvery surface. She let her breath leak out gradually, fighting the impulse to let it go in one burst and grab another breath. Don't let it out, she told herself sternly. There's no more!

When she'd gone up about thirty feet, Nancy did run out of air. She continued to struggle desperately toward the surface, the blood roaring in her ears, red dots dancing across her eyes. She was ready to pass out!

Just as the world was closing in on her and turning black, Nancy broke the surface. Her head thrown back, she gulped in air. Weakly she waved at the boat, bobbing fifty yards away. Her chest burned, her arms and legs weighed a ton, but she was alive!

"It couldn't have been sabotage," Nancy insisted for the third time. She hugged her long legs to her chest, a towel draped around her shoulders. "No one knew we were going diving."

"She's right," Tommy agreed. "It was just faulty equipment. I should have checked it more carefully." His usually cheerful face was drawn. Nancy could see he blamed himself for her accident.

"Stop worrying about it. I'm really fine, just a little shaken," she repeated.

"I can't *believe* I left you alone!" he insisted miserably. "But I wanted to check out that cave. When I came back and found you gone . . ." His voice trailed off.

"Bet you thought she was eaten by a shark," George joked.

Tommy gave her a stricken look.

Bess put her arm around him sympathetically. "Nancy's okay," she said. "She can hold her breath longer than anyone I know."

A quiet and thoughtful group headed back to the dock. Nancy turned the case over in her mind.

It looked as though she was on the wrong track, she had to admit to herself. She had been asked to find a missing painter and a missing painting, not to investigate a death. Looking back, Nancy wondered all of a sudden if the note saying that Nicholas was murdered had been written to send her in the wrong direction.

Sasha came over and sat next to Nancy. "Will you come by later to see our rehearsal? It should end around four-thirty or five. After that I can give you a dance lesson."

Nancy nodded absently.

"Are you thinking about the accident?" he asked sympathetically.

Nancy shook her head. "I'm thinking about the connection between Christopher and Nicholas," she said. "And about Bob Tercero. I'm tempted to think that he's pushing me in the wrong direction."

"So you think he is the bad guy? He is trying to keep you from finding Christopher?" Sasha asked.

"I don't know," Nancy said. "He was actually pretty helpful when we were talking about Christopher. After all, it would hurt the gallery enormously if Christopher doesn't turn up. And a lot of Bob's job involves working with the Scotts. The thing that is so confusing is the way he talks about Nicholas."

"Speaking of strange reactions," Sasha said, "Megan was very sure that the *Vanity* does not exist."

Nancy nodded. "You're getting good at this," she said.

"A compliment from you about my detective work?" Sasha asked. "That means a lot to me."

Nancy blushed, deciding to ignore his remark. "Back to Megan," she began. "Does her reaction mean she *has* seen the painting and was just covering it up? Or was she being sincere? Maybe it's true that Christopher Scott painted nothing but landscapes.

"But if there is no *Vanity,* then Bob Tercero made it up. And why would he do that?" Nancy asked, frustrated. As the boat pulled into the dock, she decided to pay another visit to the gallery manager.

Nancy, Bess, and George headed back to Eloise's house to shower and change. They made turkey sandwiches for lunch before heading over to the Nisus Gallery to talk with Bob Tercero.

When they walked into the gallery, Bess took George on a quick tour.

"Look at this. Isn't it beautiful?" Bess asked George, gazing at Christopher Scott's large pink canvas.

George shrugged. "It's too pink for me," she replied.

Bob Tercero came into the room.

"I thought I heard familiar voices," he said. "You're back sooner than I expected."

Nancy introduced George to Bob. He led them down the hall into his office, one door before Cynthia's.

"Is Mrs. Gray here?" George asked.

"No," Bob replied. "She's seldom here."

"We came back to fill you in on our trip to the Scotts' place," Nancy cut in. She watched Tercero carefully, waiting for his reaction to her next comment. "We found out there is no *Vanity* painting," she said.

Tercero looked at her blankly. "What are you talking about? Of course there is."

"Not according to Megan Archer," she said.

"Who?"

"Megan Archer, Nicholas's girlfriend," Nancy replied. "Haven't you ever met his girlfriend?"

The confusion on Tercero's face cleared. "Oh, right, the new one. She's been in town only a few months," he said, dismissing her. "Don't pay any attention to her. She doesn't know anything. Of course there's a *Vanity*."

"Megan seems very sure you're wrong about that," Nancy persisted. "There's no sign of it at his studio. In fact, there's no sign of a working artist anywhere in the house or the studio."

"The *Vanity* exists," Bob repeated, a tolerant smile on his face. "I not only bought it, I was there when Chris was painting it."

Now it was Nancy's turn to look taken aback.

"You still don't believe me?" Tercero asked. "Wait, I have proof." He took a binder out of his desk and began paging through it. "This is Scott's catalog," he explained. He turned the binder around, "Here. This is a picture of the *Vanity*."

"Look at that!" Bess exclaimed. "It really does exist."

On the page was a photo and a description of the *Vanity*. The picture showed a canvas of a girl in a white nightgown seated in front of a mirror. Long red curls cascaded down her shoulders, obscuring all but the side of her face.

Nancy looked at Bob. "You were there when he was painting it?" she asked. "So why did you tell me you didn't know who the model was?"

Bob seemed startled by the question. Then he shrugged. "Well, I didn't really *know* her. She was a model, a professional from New York. I know that much," he explained. "She was dating Nicholas."

"You have no idea where we could find her?" George broke in.

Bob seemed faintly alarmed. "No, I have no idea where you could find her. Listen, forget it and her, okay? The painting's not that important. Really," he said earnestly. "It would have been nice if you found it, but I don't want you to waste your time. The important thing is to find Christopher. Once you do that, I'll ask him about the *Vanity* myself."

Bob Tercero was up to some trick, Nancy thought, annoyed. Suddenly he had become adamant that the painting was unimportant and was refusing to help her find the model.

"Well, if you think it's not important, then there's no point in looking for it," Nancy said, standing up. "After all, you were the one who asked me to find it in the first place. We won't take up any more of your time with it."

"Find Christopher," Bob repeated. "I promise you, Nicholas told me he was working on a painting the day of the accident. There must be some trace of it somewhere."

Nancy and her friends left the gallery in silence. So far, Nancy thought, she knew only two people who had been involved in the Scotts' personal lives. Now she knew of a third person, the red-haired model. Nancy decided she was going to find the girl. Maybe she'd get some answers from her.

"What a creep!" Bess exclaimed when the girls were back in Nancy's car.

"He's definitely hiding something," George agreed. "But what?"

"I'm not sure," Nancy said thoughtfully. "He wanted me to look for Chris and the painting, only he doesn't want me looking too hard. And then there's the question of Nicholas being murdered. Maybe the girl in the painting could help us. It seems she knew both Bob and the Scotts."

"But how do we find her?" Bess asked. "The picture won't help. You can barely see her face."

"Modeling agencies," George piped up. "Didn't you hear him say she was a professional model?"

Bess practically jumped with excitement. "We're going to modeling agencies!" she exclaimed. "You always hear stories about girls walking into those places and becoming super-stars!"

"Well, let's try calling first," Nancy suggested, keeping a straight face. "I don't know if we have time to go into New York City and pound the pavement."

Seeing Bess's disappointed face, George patted her cousin's shoulder consolingly. "Let's stop by Jetstream," she suggested to Nancy. "I know they have a Manhattan phone book in their office."

"My aunt has one, too," Nancy said. "Sorry, George, no time to see Gary."

"Oh, well, I tried," George said, and laughed at herself on the way back to Eloise Drew's.

"George, you look up the numbers," Nancy suggested. "I'll start calling."

"What are you going to say?"

"That I'm looking for a redhead," Nancy replied. "Someone who has experience modeling for painters. I'd guess that's pretty unusual for a professional model."

"It's a long shot," George said. "What if they want details, like what you're paying?"

"I read somewhere that models make thou-sands," Bess warned.

"Bess, George, I'm not hiring the girl!" Nancy exclaimed. "I just want to find her."

As she made call after call, Nancy realized George's skepticism made sense. Over and over she was told: no redheads, no portrait sittings.

Finally she got the booking agent for the Unique Agency on the phone. A red-haired model was no problem, she was told. Then Nancy explained she wanted the model for a painter.

"No way!" the agent yelled. "We don't work with painters anymore. The last time we sent a girl out to pose for a painting, we never saw her again!"

Chapter

Seven

NANCY CAUGHT HER BREATH. A missing model? She pressed the woman for details.

"No," the woman said, laughing. "She wasn't a redhead. She was Nigerian. She was posing for some young hotshot painter in Manhattan, and last I heard, they were married. But the real reason we don't work with painters is that they tie up our models for long periods of time. We can make more money on shorter assignments."

Seeing Nancy's disappointed face as she hung up, Bess suggested, "I could do some calling, Nan."

Nancy shook her head. "I think we have to find another way." She looked at her watch. "Oh, no!

Is it really four-thirty? I promised Sasha I'd go and watch his rehearsal, but it's almost over."

"Brush your hair and get out of here quick," Bess teased. "You don't want to be late!"

Nancy threw Bess a withering look but did gather her things and jump into their rental car.

The dance institute was housed for the summer in an old school that the Hamptons Cultural Society had taken over. It had been renovated, and now it contained a stage, auditorium, and rehearsal and dressing rooms.

The auditorium at the institute was empty when Nancy walked in. She'd missed Sasha's rehearsal, she thought, sitting down heavily on one of the chairs. She was doing it again—getting so involved in a mystery that she was missing out on everything else!

As Nancy sat there, Sasha's partner, Marina, walked into the room. Marina was a young ballerina from the Soviet Union who had come to the institute with Sasha.

At first Nancy had thought that the lovely black-haired dancer might be in love with Sasha and might resent Nancy because of the attention Sasha paid to her. But later she had decided she was wrong about Marina. Marina's first love was ballet. The two Soviets danced together beautifully, but that was all. When it came to Sasha, Marina was all business.

"Hi, Nancy," she called. "Looking for Sasha?"

Nancy nodded and Marina's lithe body disappeared into the back.

A few seconds later Sasha walked into the auditorium, wearing black tights and a white T-shirt. The strong muscles in his arms were flexed as he held each end of a towel that was thrown around his neck.

"Sasha, I'm sorry I'm late—" Nancy began.

Sasha shook his head, waving away her apology. He took her arm lightly. "Ready for that dance lesson?" he asked, giving her a peck on the cheek.

"I'm hardly dressed for it," she protested, laughing.

His eyes surveyed her with approval. "Nice lightweight shirt, loose cotton pants," he said. "Take off your sandals and you'll be perfect." He looked into her eyes. "I'm not letting you get away, Nancy Drew."

Phew! Nancy thought, every time she was with this guy, she couldn't think straight!

Sasha led her into a rehearsal room and put on some music. Then he sat in the middle of the dance floor. "Come on," he invited. "We'll warm up so you don't pull any muscles."

Nancy sat on the floor beside him, obediently following his orders. As she stretched, she felt her body relax.

"I thought ballet dancers warmed up at the barre," Nancy said, pointing to the long polished wood rail running along one mirrored wall.

"We do, but unless you are experienced, the barre is not going to get you very warm.

"I wasn't going to give you a real ballet lesson," Sasha continued. "I have learned some great modern dance and jazz moves from some of the American dancers here. I was going to teach you little pieces of each."

"You mean I won't get to float around in pointe shoes and a tutu?" Nancy said, pretending to be disappointed.

"No," Sasha replied, taking Nancy seriously. "You need years of training for that. Have you ever taken ballet?"

Nancy shook her head.

"Then we will stay away from the barre and stick with something fun. Now, breathe out," Sasha directed. "Just like in aerobics. Don't bounce when you reach for your toes. Close your eyes and just *stretch.*"

When Nancy had loosened up, Sasha pulled her to her feet.

"Let's dance." He came up behind her, showing her how to move her arms. "This gesture is from modern dance," he explained. "It's from a piece by a famous choreographer. It's very sensuous."

Nancy, feeling the warmth of his muscular body behind her, had to force her mind back to listen to his directions.

"And this is a jazz step," he continued. "Three steps toward me, now bend back around my arm—like this." He pulled her smoothly down into a dip. "Jazz is the best!"

"What about ballet?" Nancy murmured, her head against his arm. His rock-hard biceps held her up effortlessly. It felt wonderful!

"Ballet doesn't have this freedom," Sasha declared. "Jazz has wonderful emotion." He spun her around until she was wrapped in his embrace, facing him. He held her that way for a moment before releasing her. "Jazz is made for a man and a woman."

They danced in the center of the empty hall, Nancy laughing at her inexperience. "You are wonderful," he assured her, twirling her around. "You have natural grace. Are you sure you have never had a lesson?"

"Just tap," she explained, "and karate."

"Then we should be doing floor exercises, or leaps," Sasha said.

Nancy rolled her eyes in mock horror. "I don't think I'm ready to roll around on the floor today," she said. "Let's stick to the basics."

Sasha's face clouded. "You still don't trust me, do you?"

Nancy felt bad. She hadn't meant to sound that way. "Of course I trust you," she replied, keeping her tone light. As soon as she said it, she knew it was true. She *did* trust Sasha. It was her own feelings she couldn't trust!

"Then here is something very basic," Sasha said. His strong hands grasped her waist. "Put your hands on mine." He lifted her easily, high above his head, swinging around in a circle.

"Basic ballet," he murmured as he eased her back down, sliding her body against his.

"Well," Nancy began, her gaze locked on his, her head whirling. "We'll certainly be a hit at the Lobster Tank if we try this maneuver there!"

"Then we should," he said, holding her tightly.

Nancy swallowed hard. Sasha's face was inches from hers. "Sasha, I . . ." she began.

Sasha's eyes searched Nancy's, a troubled look on his face. He reached out and touched his finger to her lips. "Do not tell me you will never dance with me again, Nancy."

Nancy had a sudden urge to comfort him. She pushed it aside with difficulty. "Sasha," she said, smiling despite herself, "thanks for the lesson." She squeezed his arm and pulled away gently. "I think that's enough for today."

Nancy saw Sasha again in a couple of hours. Cynthia Gray had invited the young people to a preview of Christopher Scott's show. Both new and old works were on display. A couple of New York's major art critics had also been invited. Cynthia had hoped that all the publicity would tempt Scott to make an appearance, but there was no sign of the painter.

Nancy spotted Bob Tercero talking with some very glamorous-looking women. He saw Nancy looking at him and smiled brightly.

Nancy smiled back, but Bob didn't see because he had already turned his attention back to his guests. Nancy circled the room alone, examining the Scott paintings on display. One was the large pink canvas she had seen earlier. Another was small, a seascape with boats, and Nancy's favorite was a bold blue-and-white rendering of an empty beach, which had been painted a year earlier.

Nancy's attention was caught by this painting because it appeared to be very simple, just a beach, waves, and sky. But there was something magical about it, something that made her want to walk into the scene. The beach sparkled, the waves glistened, and for a moment Nancy was sure the water was actually moving. As she stood staring at it, Nancy understood for the first time why Christopher Scott was considered a great painter.

She looked for Sasha, who had gone to get a soft drink, and saw him talking with George and Gary and a woman she didn't know. The woman, dressed in a skintight red suit, couldn't keep her eyes off Sasha. George spotted Nancy and excused herself to join her friend.

"She's the wife of someone important," George said, referring to the woman in red. "Poor Sasha. She's so boring!"

Nancy smiled. "Well, then, we should stay far away from her, shouldn't we?" Then she took a second look. The woman was resting her hand on Sasha's arm. "She certainly seems interested in Sasha, though," Nancy added under her breath.

"Don't worry, she's much too old for him," George said. She grinned slyly at Nancy.

"George!" Nancy was annoyed for a moment. She wished her friends wouldn't tease her about Sasha.

"Okay, okay," George said. "Sorry. I promise I won't mention either of you again this evening."

Nancy and George moved around the room, listening to conversations, trying to pick up any new information about Christopher Scott.

"Everyone is speculating about the show and wondering whether Scott will show up," George said. "Seems like the whole town knows something's up."

"I noticed that," Nancy said slowly. "People are trading stories about the last time they saw him. You know, I think the most recent 'encounter' I heard about was from some woman who said she'd seen him in the supermarket last fall."

"Last fall!" George exclaimed. "That was almost a year ago!"

Nancy nodded. She guided George over to a corner where three well-dressed men were talking about the painter.

"I guess he can't bear to be here without Nicholas," one of them suggested. "I hear he's vowed to give up painting forever."

"Just between us," the second man said, "I don't know if that's such a tragedy. Christopher's work has been slipping lately. The new paintings I've seen in the last six months are very dull.

Look at what they've got here tonight! The only piece worth mentioning is that blue-and-white canvas, and that one was done almost a year ago, I think."

Nancy saw Cynthia heading toward the group. She was dressed in gray silk, with large diamond drop earrings hanging almost to her shoulders.

"If he *has* given up painting, this is a final farewell," the third man replied, "and we should see his unfinished work. As you know, Christopher was famous for starting a canvas and not finishing it for years."

Cynthia floated up to the group. "Are you having a good time?" she asked them. "What do you think of the new works?"

The three men complimented the new paintings, and then the third man repeated his comment about Scott's unfinished work.

Cynthia bristled. "Christopher Scott is far from retired," she assured them. "And as for his unfinished work, I can assure you he's finishing everything now."

The first man stepped in smoothly and suggested something to eat, and the group moved away. Nancy thought back to her trip to Scott's studio. She hadn't seen a single painting, finished or unfinished, in the whole place! Scott's work had simply disappeared—the *Vanity* and all the unfinished paintings he was so famous for.

Sasha and Gary came over to join the girls.

"You abandoned me," Gary said, slipping his

arm fondly around George. "But I forgive you. Can I get you a soda?"

Nancy turned to Sasha and yawned.

"How can you be bored with me?" he protested, grinning. "I haven't even said anything!"

Nancy laughed. "It's not you at all," she said. "I guess it's been a long day."

"Well, a walk in the fresh air should wake you up," Sasha suggested.

"George?" Nancy said, turning back to her friend. She thought it might be wise to invite her to come along. But to her surprise, George and Gary had slipped away and were nowhere to be seen. Bess was across the room with Tommy, talking with a young painter outfitted in black from head to toe.

"Why not?" Nancy agreed, since she couldn't think of any good excuse. Besides, a walk on the beach sounded terrific. She and Sasha hopped into her car and headed for the ocean.

When they got out of the car, Nancy gathered her full cotton skirt in one hand and slipped off her shoes. She picked her way over the sand, her feet sinking luxuriously into it with each step.

Nancy reached the waterline and sat down, picking up handfuls of white sand and pouring them back out in little piles. The wind carried the tangy smell of salt and fish across the beach.

Nancy leaned back on her hands and dug her toes in the sand. "You're right," she said, "I feel much better now."

She looked around her. The setting was romantic. The moon was high in a clear, dark sky. The waves crashed on the sand, slipping up the shore almost to where Nancy and Sasha were sitting.

"This is perfect," she said, smiling up at Sasha. He put his arm around her in response.

This time Nancy didn't pull away. She sat there, wrapped securely in his embrace, listening to the waves.

At last Nancy took a deep breath. She had to make a decision, she thought for the millionth time, and it might as well be now.

"I don't know what to say, Sasha," she began, afraid to meet his eyes. "I'm all confused. I don't know how I feel about you, or how I feel about Ned. I hope you don't hate me."

"Hate you?" Sasha asked.

"Don't stop me, I need to say this," Nancy continued, keeping her eyes on the ocean. "Ned and I, we don't have any vows, but we trust each other. We have a very good, long-standing relationship, and I feel disloyal to him when I'm with you."

"So why are you with me?" he asked quietly.

Nancy hugged her legs. Why *was* she? she asked herself. Finally, she turned to face him.

"Because I have fun with you. I'm happy being with you," she said, feeling vulnerable. "And I don't know what it means or what to do about it."

Sasha laughed and squeezed her affectionately. "Look at me, Nancy," he said, tilting her chin toward him with his finger. "Relax. Don't worry about this. You have time to make up your mind."

Nancy smiled gratefully. Sasha, suddenly shy, cast around for something else to talk about.

"What's that?" he asked suddenly, pointing to a dark object in the sand.

Nancy followed his finger. "This?" she asked, picking it up. "It's a horseshoe crab."

Sasha was dubious. "It looks like a prehistoric bug," he said.

"They are a little scary looking," she agreed. Seeing the distasteful look on Sasha's face, she grinned. "It's just the shell, silly."

It was getting late, Nancy realized, and it was time to go home. The two of them walked back to the car hand in hand. Nancy felt at peace. Sasha was right, they did have all the time in the world.

"You want some music?" Sasha asked, opening the glove compartment to look for a tape.

"There's a tape in already," Nancy replied.

Sasha pulled out a tape from the slot. "Do you know what it is?" he asked, turning it over. "There's no label."

Nancy shrugged, her eyes on the road. "Put it in and see."

Sasha pushed the tape in. There was a quiet hiss. Then suddenly a distorted voice floated out of the speakers.

"If you don't want to end up like Scott," the voice warned, "you'll stick to the murder and stay away from the *Vanity!*"

Chapter

Eight

SASHA EJECTED THE TAPE in alarm. "I remember when this was supposed to be a nice, safe mystery," he said grimly.

"It does get weirder and weirder," Nancy agreed. She filled Sasha in on her conversation with Bob Tercero and the comments she'd overheard at the party.

"What are we going to do?" he asked. "We can't just let this guy keep threatening you."

"It's the first threat," Nancy said, trying to think it through.

"What about the note you got at the dance club?" Sasha reminded her.

"The note seemed to me to be an attempt to help, some kind of a clue."

Sasha looked doubtful. "So you think they are from two different people?"

"That's the problem," Nancy admitted, drumming her fingers thoughtfully on the steering wheel. "They could be from two different people, but I doubt it. Both messages refer to Scott's murder, and nothing else we've uncovered so far has anything to do with murder."

"But why would the same person try to help you once, and then threaten you the next time?"

"That's what we have to find out. What made our mysterious tipper change his or her mind about our investigation?"

After assuring him she would call him the next day, Nancy dropped Sasha off and headed home.

She was back to murder, Nancy realized as she climbed into bed, and back to Nicholas Scott. Every time she decided she was finished with Nicholas, something pointed to him again. Unless . . . unless, Nancy thought excitedly, maybe she'd misunderstood the first note.

Maybe someone was trying to tell her that *Christopher* Scott was murdered! Sitting up in bed, Nancy tried to reason this out.

If Christopher Scott had been murdered, who would be leaving clues for Nancy? The killer? It didn't seem likely. But if it was just someone who knew too much and was scared to come forward, why would that person leave a threatening note?

Why would anyone kill Christopher Scott? And when would it have happened? He had been working the day Nicholas died, so he would have to have been killed between then and Nicholas's funeral.

"But if Christopher was killed," Nancy said out loud, "what happened to the body?" She stared into the darkness. She knew that murder was hard to cover up. Bodies didn't vanish without a trace.

And then there was the question of motive. The bad guy, as Sasha put it, seemed to be Bob Tercero. But why? He should want Christopher alive and working. He made money from Christopher's paintings, and he really seemed to want Nancy to find Christopher.

All right, so maybe it was ridiculous to think Christopher had been murdered. The whole case just didn't make sense! Nancy thought, tossing restlessly.

This last clue, the warning on the tape, definitely tied the missing *Vanity* painting to the mystery. Nancy would have to find the redhaired model and the painting, she vowed, and the sooner the better. She'd get to work on it first thing in the morning.

With that, she finally fell into a troubled sleep.

The next morning Nancy met Bess and George at breakfast with Aunt Eloise.

"Good morning," she greeted her aunt with a peck on the cheek.

Eloise Drew always reminded Nancy of her father, Eloise's brother Carson. She was tall and slender like her brother, but younger—her shin-

ing brown hair was still untouched by gray.
Eloise was a teacher, and a very independent
woman. She treated Nancy with warmth and
affection but rarely fussed over her or tried to run
her life. Nancy loved spending time with her.

"Hi, guys." Nancy turned to her friends. "You
two must have come in late—I didn't even hear
you. Do I have a story for you!"

"I have one first," Bess declared, ready to
burst. "Someone wants to paint my picture!

"Did you see that guy I was talking to last
night?" she continued. "Well, his name is Doug
Coggins, and he's a famous New York artist. I
must have talked to him for an hour! He said I
inspire him and he wants me to model for him."

"That's the third time she's told *that* story,"
George said, smiling tolerantly at her cousin.
"Once for me, once for Eloise, and now for you."

Bess was lost in her daydreams and barely
noticed when George refocused her attention on
Nancy. "What's up? Is it the mystery or Sasha?"

Nancy decided to ignore the teasing tone in
George's voice. "The mystery. I got another
message last night. And this one wasn't quite so
helpful."

She filled them in. When she was finished,
everyone was quiet.

"Well?" Nancy asked. "Someone say something."

"What do you want us to say?" Eloise asked.
"If Nicholas really was murdered, this case
sounds quite dangerous, but you know that al-

ready. You'll ignore us if we say it's too dangerous. And you're *always* careful, right?"

Nancy laughed. "Do you guys want to do a
little poking around with me?" she asked George
and Bess. "I want to talk to everyone even
remotely connected with this thing. One of them
has got to be sending me these messages."

"How can you be sure?" her aunt Eloise asked.

"Well, who knows I'm investigating?" she
asked. "Cynthia, Bob, and Megan know. No one
else does—not even the police. And one fact I
keep running into is that very few people knew
the Scotts. Some of the guests at the party last
night said they hadn't seen Christopher in
months! If there is foul play involved, I'm sure
one of those three knows about it."

"Tommy knows you're investigating, too,"
George commented.

"George!" Bess protested. "Tommy's not a
suspect!"

"I didn't say he was," she said mildly. "But
you may recall, when we were investigating
Jetstream we had to remember that Gary could
be involved. I'd say this was pretty similar."

Bess sighed and turned to Nancy. "So you're
going to try to root out the person who's been
threatening you?" she asked. "What are you
going to say to him or her?"

"That someone wants me off the case," Nancy
replied. "And I want to know why. I won't say
what was in the messages, though."

"Good idea," her aunt said approvingly. "That way maybe the person will slip and mention something he or she shouldn't know. Nancy, I certainly hope you *will* be careful."

"I will be," Nancy promised as she stood up.

The three girls got into their rental car and drove to the Nisus Art Gallery. Cynthia Gray was there, checking the room for the official opening the next night. The receptionist, Cecilia, was working arranging flowers under Cynthia's discriminating eye. While the girls waited for Cynthia, Nancy spotted Bob Tercero and pulled him aside.

She launched into her story about the messages. To her surprise, Bob seemed very concerned.

"You should watch yourself," he said. "We want to find Christopher very badly but not at your expense. Is there anything I can do to help?"

"I don't think so," Nancy said. "But I'll let you know if there is."

"Listen," he said, "Cynthia's going to be at the gallery for the next two days preparing for the show, so I have the next two days off. I'll be at the opening, but otherwise, you can reach me at home." Bob scrawled his address and phone number on a scrap of paper.

"If I can help in any way, please let me know," he said, shoving the paper into Nancy's hand.

Finally Cynthia took a break and ushered the girls into her office.

"I'm shocked!" she exclaimed when Nancy had finished her story. "A serious threat?"

Nancy nodded. "Serious enough. You have no idea who it could be?"

"I'm afraid I don't, but I must say I don't like the idea of your being threatened on my account. Maybe you should drop the case."

"I thought you were worried about Christopher!" Bess burst out. "Nancy can't stop now."

"I *am* worried about Chris," Cynthia said gently, "but I don't want anyone hurt. I'm also hoping that he'll come to the gallery tomorrow night. There's been an enormous amount of publicity about the show. It would be just like him to appear in time for the opening. He's very impulsive."

"I don't want to get hurt, either," Nancy replied. "Maybe I should wait until tomorrow to see if he does come back."

Nancy and her friends headed out of town.

"You're not really going to give up, are you?" George asked.

"Of course not," Nancy declared as she slowed her car to a stop at a red light. "But if Cynthia wants us to think Scott might show up tomorrow night, I'm not going to argue with her."

"Nancy, you don't suspect her?" Bess asked defensively. "She's the one who called you in the first place, and she *is* Tommy's mother."

"Bess, I have to be objective. I honestly don't think she ran out and killed the Scotts, if that's what you're asking," Nancy replied lightly. "I just think it's odd that she wants us to drop the case. Maybe she really is worried about me—I just want to make sure, that's all."

Nancy put on her left blinker and turned into the driveway to Megan Archer's house. "Last stop for the moment," she said cheerfully. "Then we go look for our model."

No one answered Nancy's continuous ringing at the door. "Well, I guess she's at work," she said, turning to the cousins. "What do you want to do now?"

"What are we doing here?" George asked.

"Megan insisted there was no *Vanity* painting," Nancy explained. "Now we know for sure that there is one. If Bob Tercero is right, and the *Vanity* was hanging in the Scotts' house, I'm sure Megan knew it, too."

"So it could be worthwhile to take a look around her house?" George asked.

"Then let's not give up so easily," Bess said. She slid her hands along the top of the door frame. "Maybe there's a key around here somewhere."

They found a key to the house inside a potted plant on the porch and went inside.

"Anybody home?" Nancy called. Getting no answer, the girls fanned out. "Look carefully," Nancy warned. "We don't want to disturb anything. Just look for any clue to the painting."

Nancy went upstairs and started with Megan's

room. Quickly she sifted through the items lying around on the girl's dresser and opened the drawers. Then she went to the closet.

In the back of the closet was a pile of clothes. Sticking out from under all of them, Nancy could see the corner of a gray canvas drop cloth.

"Bess, George!" she cried in excitement. "Come quick!" Nancy pointed to the pile. "Look," she said. She pulled the clothes away to expose the drop cloth. It was wrapped around something rectangular and flat. "Help me get it out."

George and Nancy dragged the object out of the closet.

Nancy pulled away the canvas and exposed a stunning portrait of a red-haired girl.

It was the *Vanity!*

Chapter

Nine

It's BEAUTIFUL!" Bess gasped.

The painting certainly was magnificent, Nancy thought. The photograph Bob Tercero had shown her had been clear, but it had failed to capture the luminous quality of the girl's skin, the deep, fiery color of her hair, or the way the white nightgown she wore seemed to shimmer.

The subject looked as though she had been frozen in the act of fixing her hair. One hand was raised over her head, and in it there was a long, thin silver object. Nancy wasn't sure what it was, but she was sure of one thing: The man who had painted this picture was a great artist.

"But what's it doing *here?*" Bess asked after a moment.

"Especially since Megan told me there was no *Vanity* painting," Nancy added. "But I think we're about to find out. I just heard the door."

"Hello?" Megan's voice called nervously.

"We're here," George answered, appearing in the bedroom doorway. "I think you'd better come up."

"Who are you?" Megan asked angrily, taking the stairs two at a time. "And just what do you think you're doing in my . . ." Her voice died away as she saw Nancy and the painting. Crossing the room, she sank down onto her bed, facing the three girls.

"You said there was no painting," Nancy said quietly.

Megan couldn't meet Nancy's eyes. "You broke into my house," she accused Nancy weakly. "I thought we were friends."

"I thought you were being honest with me," Nancy replied. "But you lied about the *Vanity.*"

"I couldn't bear to part with it," Megan said. "It was Nicholas's favorite. Toward the end, he spent a lot of time just staring at it. I think he was very proud."

"But the model is one of his old girlfriends," Bess said, puzzled. "Why would you want a painting of her?"

Megan's brown eyes flashed. "She wasn't a girlfriend. Just someone he knew slightly."

Nancy persisted. "It was his favorite? Why did he single the *Vanity* out as his favorite of all of Christopher's paintings?"

"What are you talking about?" Megan asked. "This isn't Christopher's painting. Nicholas painted this."

Nancy looked at the painting again, astonished. No one had ever mentioned Nicholas could paint. And certainly not like this!

"Of course he could paint," Megan said when Nancy voiced her surprise. "He was very messy, he got it all over his clothes and in his hair—"

"Have you ever seen anything he painted?" Nancy interrupted.

"I just told you—he painted this!"

"Bob Tercero said Christopher sold the *Vanity* to the gallery," George said.

"That's a lie," Megan declared. "It was never his to sell. Nicholas asked me to take care of it in case anything happened to him, and that's what I'm doing."

"If anything happened to him?" Nancy repeated. "Didn't that seem odd to you?"

"He always said things like that," Megan said.

Nancy was torn. She didn't know whether to trust Megan, but she was sure she didn't trust Bob Tercero. All she had was his word that the *Vanity* belonged to the gallery.

"I'm going to leave the painting with you, Megan," Nancy said finally. "I'll go back to the gallery and see if there's some proof to the claim that they own it. But I need a picture of it. Do you have a camera?"

"A Polaroid," Megan offered. "Will that do?"

"That's perfect," Nancy said as Megan left to get the camera.

Nancy took a picture of the painting and walked down to the front door. "Megan, will you promise to keep the painting safe until I find out what's going on?" she asked.

"That's why I have it," Megan replied softly. "Because Nicholas wanted me to take care of it."

On the drive back home, Bess and George tried to convince Nancy to put the mystery aside and go with them to the beach.

"Just for an hour!" Bess pleaded. "I finally pried George away from Gary so we could all be together. We can discuss the case, I promise."

"Okay, okay." Nancy gave in, laughing. "Can we stop at home and get our suits, or do you want to go like this?"

"I'll let you stop at home only if you promise not to read your mail or answer the telephone," Bess threatened with a grin.

The girls changed and gathered their beach gear. It was the first time in a while that they'd had time to relax and talk alone. The beach was crowded, but they found space to spread out their towels. The first thing they did was to slather sunscreen on their bodies.

"I don't know how these people stand it," Bess said, looking at the magnificent modern houses that dotted the beach above the vegetation line. "Imagine having all these strangers lying around in your front yard."

George snorted. "Like us, you mean?" she asked as she lay back and closed her eyes.

Bess laughed. Then she put on an elaborately casual tone of voice. "Did I tell you Tommy and I are going out alone tonight? Without anyone else?"

"You mean, like on a date?" George asked.

"Not *like* a date!" Bess corrected her. "It is a date. Our first official one. All the others involved casts of thousands." Smiling smugly, she continued to rub sunscreen onto her arms.

"That's great, Bess!" Nancy said.

"Anyway, I need advice on what to wear," Bess told them. "Something devastatingly gorgeous." She began to look a little worried. "Actually, now that I think about it, I should be shopping right now!"

"Hold on," Nancy said. "Where are you going?"

"Uh, I'm not sure. Pizza and a movie, I think." Bess closed her eyes in rapture. "I have butterflies in my stomach! I haven't been this nervous about a date in ages."

"Pizza and a movie isn't that big a deal," George said dryly. "You can leave the evening gown in the closet, I think. Relax, Bess!"

Nothing could put a damper on Bess's mood. She babbled and commented on everything she saw. Nancy tried to concentrate on Bess's bright chatter, but the mystery kept intruding. She was itching to find out if the gallery owned the painting, but she wasn't anxious to run into Cynthia or Bob.

"Nancy, did you *hear* me?" Bess asked, exasperated.

Nancy looked up guiltily.

"I said, look at the sailboats. They're really racing in this wind." Bess sighed. "Honestly, when you're on a case, you're hopeless!"

Nancy waited until just before closing time to go back to the gallery. She was in luck. When she got there, Cynthia and Bob were nowhere in sight. Nancy went over to the reception desk and reintroduced herself to Cecilia.

"Yes, I remember you," the girl responded. "Cynthia told me to help you in any way I can. You just missed her, by the way."

Nancy pretended to be disappointed. "And I really needed to talk to her. Would you mind if I left her a note?"

Cecilia handed Nancy a pad of note paper.

"It's a long note," Nancy said hastily. "And I don't want to hang over your desk while I write. Do you mind if I go into one of the offices in the back to write it?"

"No problem," the girl said agreeably. "I've got to hang around for another half hour anyway."

Nancy went down the hall and slipped into Bob's office. She had seen the account books there the last time she came. If the Nisus Gallery really had bought the *Vanity* painting, she should be able to find proof of the payment in one of the books.

Nancy pulled down the ledgers and paged through them, checking each payment to Christopher Scott carefully. They were recorded neatly, each one for fifteen thousand dollars. There was no entry for the *Vanity*. Nancy checked again, but she had been right the first time. The portrait wasn't listed.

So Megan had been telling the truth, she thought. Bob had lied. But why would he want that particular painting so badly? It hadn't even been painted by Christopher, according to Megan.

As Nancy flipped the pages, she noticed something else. Tommy had told Bess that nothing at Nisus sold for less than twenty thousand dollars. But according to the ledger, a number of paintings had sold for much less, as little as five thousand dollars each. Nancy examined the entries carefully. None of them was Christopher Scott's. But, she realized, all of the cheaper paintings were sold to the same place—ART Inc.

Nancy went back to where the artists' commissions were listed. Each of the payments to the artists whose work was sold to ART Inc. matched the sale price exactly. So the Nisus Gallery hadn't made any money on those paintings at all!

There were other payments to ART Inc., she saw, like consultants' fees, frames, and supplies. ART Inc. must be another gallery. That could explain why the prices were so low. Was it usual for one gallery to sell paintings to another at cost?

Nancy didn't know. From what she understood, most of the paintings were handled on a commission basis, with no money going to the artist until the painting was actually sold. When there was an exclusive arrangement such as the one Cynthia Gray had with Christopher Scott, Nancy guessed, the gallery probably gave the artist an advance payment. That must explain the constant payments of fifteen thousand dollars to him.

Nancy slipped the book back onto the shelf. She was curious about the accounts and the ART gallery. But that wasn't her case. None of the Scott paintings was involved.

Nancy looked through the Nisus Gallery's checkbook, studying the stubs. ART Inc. was located in the Hamptons! The address was right there.

Nancy copied down the address and slipped it into her purse. She had time to drive over there before it got dark, she thought.

Leaving a note with Cecilia for Cynthia, Nancy left the gallery and got into her car.

As she drove along, Nancy admired the old Hamptons homes with their gingerbread details on wraparound porches. Many of the houses looked Victorian. They were pretty, though not as elaborate as the sprawling modern ones in the Scotts' neighborhood.

It seemed strange that ART Inc. wasn't with

the other galleries, in the commercial part of town. Nancy's destination turned out to be a house. Maybe she had remembered the address wrong, she thought, pulling over to the side of the road. She pulled out her wallet and took a slip of paper from it.

Nancy glanced down at the paper in her hand. It had an address written on it, but not for ART Inc. What she had in her hand was Bob Tercero's address and phone number, which he had written down for her that afternoon.

Nancy's pulse quickened. According to the paper in her hand, she had pulled up in front of Bob Tercero's house.

Nancy pulled out the slip on which she had written the address for ART Inc. The addresses matched. Bob Tercero's house and ART Inc. were one and the same!

Chapter

Ten

WELL, I MIGHT AS WELL see what he has to say about this," Nancy muttered to herself. Getting out of her car, she strode up to Bob's porch and knocked at his door. There was no answer.

Things were beginning to make sense, she thought as she drove home. Bob Tercero must be selling paintings to himself at prices far below market value. The low prices meant that not only did Nisus make no money on the sales, but since the artists' fees were based on the sale prices, the artists didn't get as much as they should either.

It was probably legal, Nancy thought, but it didn't seem very ethical. How could Bob do it without Cynthia finding out? she wondered. Or was Cynthia involved? Nancy didn't like to think she could be, but then she remembered the woman telling her to drop the case.

Nancy had to decide what this new development meant. Should she do anything about it? She was uncovering a lot in her search, but none of it had anything to do with Christopher Scott's whereabouts, she thought in frustration. At least she was sure that the Nisus Gallery didn't own the *Vanity* painting, so it was all right to leave it with Megan for the moment.

Nancy drove back to her aunt's house. When she got there, she found George and Eloise sprawled out on couches in front of the television. An open box of pizza was sitting on the coffee table.

"Hi." George waved her over, a slice of pizza in her hand. "Bess is out with Tommy, and Gary's in New York City visiting his sister. Eloise and I decided to have a girls' night at home. Come join us."

"Unless you have a date," Eloise put in, exchanging an amused glance with George.

"No," Nancy said, sinking into a chair, "no date, believe it or not. Sorry to disappoint you two. Is the pizza still warm?"

"It just arrived," George said, putting a slice on a plate for Nancy. "Where have you been?"

Nancy took a few bites of pizza before telling them about her investigation at the gallery and Bob Tercero's scheme.

"Everything points everywhere *except* to Christopher Scott," Nancy remarked tiredly when she finished her story. "I just have this feeling I'm missing the most important clue. There's got to be something that ties it all together."

"Let's go over this again," her aunt suggested. "Forget Bob's company for a minute. Bob Tercero says the Nisus Gallery owns the *Vanity,* but from what you can see, it doesn't. Megan says it's impossible. Megan also says, oddly, that *Nicholas* painted the *Vanity.* Bob says he was there when Christopher was painting it, and that was before Megan had met the Scotts, anyway."

"If I can positively decide who did the painting, I could understand much more. If Nicholas Scott actually painted something that's been attributed to his uncle . . ." Nancy's voice trailed off. Something was nagging at the back of her mind. What was she missing?

"You saw the painting," her aunt Eloise's voice broke in on Nancy's thoughts. "Did it look like Christopher's work to you?"

Nancy gave up. Whatever the thought was, it was lost for the moment. "Well, yes, but I'm no art expert," she said. "Maybe I can get Tommy to look at it. He must be pretty familiar with Scott's work."

They decided to stop discussing the case and watch a movie George had rented.

"Hello!" Bess called merrily a couple of hours later. "I'm home."

"How was it?" George said, pouncing on her.

"Heavenly!" Bess exclaimed. She sat down

near the pizza. "Is that cold pizza? One of my passions."

"I thought you and Tommy went out for pizza," Nancy said, puzzled.

"We did, but I didn't eat more than half a slice. I was too nervous," Bess confessed. "So now I'm starving!"

"Forget the food," George said impatiently. "Get to the good part."

"Well . . ." Bess leaned back on the couch, a satisfied look on her face. "He kissed me!"

"During the movie?" George asked.

"Not at the movie," Bess said in disgust. "We were *watching* the movie. Later."

"When?" Nancy asked, leaning forward.

"Later," Bess repeated. "Okay, let me start from the beginning. First we had dinner at the Pizza Stop, and I didn't eat much, as I told you, but we talked about *everything*. He's really smart, you know. Then we went to the movie."

"And?" George urged.

"It was a great show. A romance. I almost cried in the end."

Eloise grinned. "Bess, stop teasing George. Tell us what happened."

"Then he drove me home. We talked about the movie on the way and kind of started talking about romance. And when we got here . . ." Bess paused, a secret smile playing about her lips.

"Go on, you know you're dying to tell us," Nancy teased.

"When we got here," Bess continued, blushing,

"he said he'd never had such a good time on a date before. And even though we'd known each other only a short time, he thought I was really special. And then he kissed me."

"Of course he did!" George exclaimed, throwing a pillow at her cousin. "What was it like?"

"What do you mean, what was it like?" Bess asked indignantly. "It's none of your business what it was like!"

"Oho!" George said. "Bess is getting touchy!"

"You just don't have the true romantic spirit," Bess said, shaking her head. "I'm going to go up to bed, and I'm not telling you anything else!" She marched up the stairs, and then paused at the top step. Turning around, she smiled down at Nancy, George, and Eloise. "But I will say this—I know I'm in love!"

The next morning Bess came down to breakfast in a turquoise blouse and swirly black skirt.

"Why so dressed up? What's the occasion?" Nancy asked.

"I'm going to be painted today. And you promised to go with me," Bess reminded her.

Nancy didn't remember promising Bess. In fact, she didn't remember discussing it, but she knew she'd been distracted lately. So Nancy drove Bess over to the painter's apartment. He lived in a large, sunny room on the top floor of an old building in town.

"Nancy, this is Doug Coggins," Bess said,

introducing the two. Nancy's eyes widened as she took in the painter's light blond hair, which was cropped a half inch from his scalp. "Doug, Nancy Drew."

Doug offered the girls some soda, then ushered Bess over to a window with north light.

"Sit on the stool," he directed her. "Now, turn your chin so the light catches the side of your face. Nancy, why don't you sit over there?"

Bess swung her legs, looking around her in delight.

Doug stood behind his canvas and studied Bess. Shaking his head, he went back to her. "I love your blouse, Bess. Would you hold your arm out so I can see more of it? And get this knee up, if you can," he said, lifting one of her legs over the other.

"This isn't very comfortable," Bess complained.

Doug shot her a warning look. "It's art, Bess. It's not supposed to be comfortable. And stop squirming around."

"I'm sorry," Bess said, freezing immediately. "It's just that no one has ever painted me before."

As Doug worked, Nancy wandered around the studio restlessly. Trying not to disturb them, Nancy kept quiet. She leafed through the books and magazines. Every so often Doug would adjust Bess's pose or tell her to hold still.

"You're awfully quiet," he commented, glancing over at Nancy.

"Oh," she said, closing the magazine on her lap. "I was trying to stay out of the way."

"Talk to me," he invited. "It helps me concentrate."

"Okay. Tell me about painting," Nancy said. "What makes a really great artist?"

"Technique, I guess," Doug replied, frowning at his canvas. "Brushwork, use of color and light. But every artist would tell you something slightly different."

"What do you think of Christopher Scott's work?"

"Fabulous! The man is a genius," he pronounced. "Bess, would you stop twitching!"

Bess grimaced. "I've been sitting here for over an hour!" she complained.

"Art takes time." Turning back to Nancy, Doug continued. "But then, I guess I'm prejudiced when it comes to Chris."

"How so?" Nancy asked.

"Well, I studied with him."

"You're kidding!" Nancy exclaimed. "I had no idea that Scott gave classes."

"Oh, he doesn't. Sometimes he takes on one student."

"Would you be familiar with his work? Enough to recognize it, I mean?" Nancy asked.

"Sure. Chris has a very distinctive style. Very original brushwork. Why?"

Nancy didn't reply immediately. "Just a theory I'm working on," she finally said.

Doug looked surprised but didn't pursue it.

Bess dropped her hand. "My arm hurts," she complained. "Are we almost finished?"

Doug sighed and put his brush down on the easel. "Okay, why don't we call it a day?"

"Great. Can I see the painting?" Bess asked, sliding off the stool.

"Not until it's done."

Bess and Doug took the empty soda glasses into the kitchenette. Nancy, left alone, sneaked around to peek at the painting.

When she saw it, it was all she could do to keep from laughing. The painting so far was an abstract arrangement of boxes and lines. It didn't look like Bess at all!

Poor Bess, all that posing for nothing, Nancy thought. Well, she was going to make sure she wasn't around when Bess saw the finished painting. She'd probably chase Doug around the room with it!

That night was the opening of the big Christopher Scott show at the Nisus Gallery. Nancy and Sasha went together, planning to meet the others there. By the time they arrived, the party was already in full swing.

The room was packed and fairly glittered with jewelry. As Nancy and Sasha pushed their way through the crowd, Nancy marveled at the obvious wealth of the guests. So this was Hamptons society! she thought. She spotted a man with a shock of white hair standing in the corner. "Isn't that the famous writer?" she asked Sasha. "Oh, what's his name?"

"I'm not even from this country. How would I know?" Sasha teased. "This place is full of famous writers. There's Bess." He pointed across the room. "Who *are* those people she's with?"

Nancy looked over and saw Doug and Bess with a group of other artists. "They must be Doug Coggins's friends," she said wryly. "They're all wearing black!"

As Nancy looked around, she noticed people were staring at her and Sasha.

"That's him!" she heard one pretty girl shriek. "The dancer. I saw him perform at the Hamptons Cultural Society Gala. He's gorgeous!"

"Is that his girlfriend?" the other one asked. "She's not so special."

Not so special! Nancy wasn't sure if she should be angry or laugh.

"How are you?" a cordial voice asked. Nancy turned to see Bob Tercero dressed impeccably in a tuxedo. "Any luck finding Chris?"

Nancy shook her head.

"Too bad," he said mildly. "Well, keep up the good work. Nice to see you."

"There's Tommy with his mother. She looks terrific," Sasha said admiringly as Bob disappeared into the crowd. "She's outshining everyone tonight. Except you, of course, Nancy." His eyes caressed Nancy's face.

Nancy blushed. He said the most outrageously flattering things—and he always made them sound so heartfelt! "I wonder if Christopher Scott is here, hiding in a corner?" she asked, changing the subject.

Tommy had just spotted them and was heading over. "Hi, guys!"

"Nancy, Tommy, how *are* you?" a rich voice broke in. Nancy turned to Emily Terner, who had joined their group.

"And Sasha Petrov, what a delight!" the petite girl said, batting her big green eyes. "Every girl in the room is watching you. I am honored just to be in your presence!" She turned to Nancy with a grin. "Have you guys been in hiding?"

Emily's huge beachside house had been the scene of a couple of memorable parties that summer. Emily seemed to know *everyone* in the Hamptons, and she was everyone's friend. Nancy didn't know her all that well, but the two girls had taken an instant liking to each other.

"Not in hiding," Nancy corrected with a smile. "Just busy."

"Well, I hope you won't be too busy to come to my house next Thursday for a pool party," Emily said, tossing her honey-colored hair over her shoulders. "Bring the whole gang."

After Nancy and Sasha had accepted the invitation, Emily turned to Tommy. "How's your brother? Where is he again?"

"Jeff's fine. He's still working in Maine, but we expect him back soon."

"Well, if he's back in time for the party, bring him, too. Where's Bess?" she asked.

Tommy blushed. "I was looking for her myself."

"Well, then, let's go find her together!"

Emily pulled Tommy away and Nancy and Sasha were left alone.

"Listen, Sasha," Nancy said, "I'm going to try to get a moment alone with Cynthia. Why don't you find George and Gary. And stay away from those silly girls!" she added as Sasha moved away.

He turned and gave her a mock salute.

Nancy made her way through the crowd to join the gallery owner. "This is a great party," she said pleasantly. "Have you seen Christopher yet?"

Cynthia shook her head. "It's still early. But the opening has been successful despite Chris's absence. I'm quite pleased with the number of out-of-town people who have come by to inquire about the show. And look at the turnout tonight!

"You know," she continued, "I had a customer today just as I was closing to get ready for the party. A stunning young woman. She insisted I let her in to see the paintings. I was sure she'd buy something, but she didn't find what she was looking for, and I couldn't interest her in anything else."

"What was she looking for?"

"Actually, it was a painting I'd never heard of," Cynthia replied. "She said it was of a girl in a white nightgown, seated at a vanity mirror with a long silver hairpin in her hand."

Nancy's heart leapt. "What did you say the girl looked like?" she pressed.

"Quite beautiful. Very delicate skin," Cynthia said. "And very long, curly red hair."

It had to be! Nancy thought excitedly. The model for the *Vanity* had been there, and she was looking for the painting!

Chapter

Eleven

SHE'D BEEN RIGHT after all, Nancy thought, congratulating herself. The painting *was* the key. Why else would the model show up now, six months after it was finished? Nancy had a chilling thought. Nicholas and Christopher Scott were both gone—could the model know it? Bob Tercero had insisted the painting had nothing to do with Christopher's disappearance, but it was obvious to her now that Bob could have lied about that, too.

Cynthia Gray didn't seem to know anything about the painting, Nancy realized. She looked around for her and saw the gallery owner had been swept back into playing hostess. Nancy decided to talk to Cynthia about the painting, and the gallery's finances, at the earliest opportunity. There was a picture of the *Vanity* in the gallery's books. If Cynthia really didn't know about the painting, then it was safe to assume Bob was keeping other things from her, too.

Nancy craned her neck, scanning the room for George, Gary, or Sasha. After a moment she spotted Gary—he was the easiest to see since he was tall.

She wove her way through the crowd until she was at his side. "Hi, Gary. Where's George?" she asked.

Gary frowned. "Emily Terner stole her away for a chat," he complained. "Where's Sasha?"

"I thought he'd be with you," Nancy confessed. "He was on his way over last time I saw him."

"Well, he never—ah! There he is," Gary said, gesturing in the direction of the buffet table.

Nancy stood on tiptoe, but she still couldn't get a clear view. "I can't see anything. What's he doing?" she asked Gary.

Gary's eyes suddenly widened. "Uh, Nancy, I think he might need to be rescued. It looks like he's been cornered by a gaggle of starstruck females." He grinned admiringly. "You know, girls just stick to him like he's magnetized. Life must be tough for that guy."

Nancy felt annoyed, and then immediately regretted it. *I have absolutely no right to be* jealous of those girls, she reminded herself. Sasha's not my boyfriend, and that's by my own choice.

Even so, Nancy couldn't shake the feeling of annoyance. Turning abruptly, she headed for the front door.

"Where are you going?" Gary called after her.

"Out for some air," Nancy replied over her shoulder. "The crowd is beginning to get to me. I'm going to walk around awhile."

But once she was outside, she sat down on the gallery's porch steps and leaned her head against the wooden rail post. It's time I stopped kidding myself, she thought. I do care about Sasha. There *is* something between us, whether I like it or not.

"Nan?" came a gentle voice behind her. Nancy swiveled her head. It was George.

"I saw you come out. Is anything wrong?" George asked, joining her friend on the steps.

Nancy shrugged. "Not really. Just the same old thing." She sighed.

"Sasha?" George guessed. Nancy nodded wordlessly.

"What are you going to do?" George asked.

"I don't know, George," Nancy replied wearily. "I just don't know what to do."

The next morning Nancy woke up with an inspiration. She thought she knew how to find the model! Bob Tercero said the girl had been dating Nicholas, and Nicholas had the reputation of being someone who was always seen in nightclubs and discos. Who would know more about local celebs than someone who was paid to write about them?

Bess was in the living room, flipping through a fashion magazine, when Nancy came downstairs.

"Where is everybody?" Nancy asked.

"Where else?" Bess answered. "Gary called and George ran off with him. She said she'd be back this afternoon. I think your aunt went shopping."

"Speaking of this afternoon, do you have Doug Coggins's telephone number?" Nancy asked. "I want to ask him to meet me at the gallery today to take a professional look at Scott's paintings."

"It's in the kitchen by the telephone," Bess replied, gazing through a fringe of blond hair. She got up and followed Nancy into the other room.

Nancy called Doug, and he agreed to meet her after lunch.

"Bess, do you want to come with me?" she asked, hanging up the phone.

"Sure. Tommy's working all day," Bess said. "Where are we going?"

"To see a gossip columnist," Nancy replied.

"Sounds like fun. Where's Sasha?" Bess asked.

"Rehearsing," Nancy said. "I thought I'd give myself a day away from him."

Bess gave her a sideways look. "Because you want to, or because you think it might be wise?"

Nancy laughed. "Oh, Bess, you know me too well! Okay, I admit I want some time to think about him without being around him. But I'd rather not talk about it, okay?"

The two girls headed down to the local newspaper office. When they got there, they ran into Susan Wexler, a reporter Nancy and her friends had met during the Jetstream mystery.

"What are you two doing here?" Susan asked.

"Looking for some information," Nancy explained. "We're here to talk to whoever writes the local gossip column."

"That would be Stephanie Marshall," Susan said, leading them to the back of the office. "She writes a very popular column called 'Stephanie Says'. . . . Is this a story? Anything I'd be interested in?"

"I'll let you know," Nancy said.

Susan took Nancy and Bess into an office and introduced them to a slender, gray-haired woman. "Promise you'll call me if this is something juicy," Susan said as she left them alone.

"We're looking for a girl," Nancy explained to Stephanie Marshall. "Someone who was in town about six months ago. I think she was dating Nicholas Scott." Briefly she described the model. "All we need is her name."

"Well, I don't remember her name, but I certainly remember her face," the columnist replied. "The girl was quite beautiful, one of Nicholas Scott's better choices—as far as looks go, I mean. I don't know her personally, but I'm sure I have clippings of her somewhere."

"Wonderful!" Bess exclaimed.

"Here's what we'll do," Stephanie said kindly. "The pictures in my photo file are alphabetical by name, or chronological, if they're of a large group. Let's try the group pictures. When did you say she was in town?"

"About six to eight months ago," Nancy repeated, remembering Bob Tercero's comment about the age of the *Vanity*.

The woman nodded. "Why don't you look through the group shots taken around that time? The captions are usually pasted on the back. If her name's not there, I can cross-reference the story in my computer and find it there."

Nancy and Bess pored through the photos. Bess found a picture of a girl who fit the description. She was dancing, her long hair flying. She held up the photo. "Is this her?" she asked.

Stephanie looked at the photo. "It sure is. And that's Nicholas."

Bess turned the photo over. "Here's the caption," she said happily. "Nicholas Scott and Diana Spitzer at Michael's Pub."

The mysterious model had an identity at last! Nancy and Bess thanked Stephanie and left the building.

"Now that we know her name, how do we find her?" Bess asked.

"Let's try the police station. We can see if anyone has heard of her.

"Diana Spitzer." Nancy repeated the name as she and Bess drove to the police station. "Why would she come back to get the *Vanity?* She could

107

have read about Nicholas's accident, but that wouldn't entitle her to the painting. Do you think she knows that Christopher's also gone."

"It's common gossip," Bess volunteered.

"But it is just gossip. And *local* gossip at that. Cynthia didn't recognize her, and neither did Megan, so she couldn't hang around here much. It worries me why she chose to come back now."

The girls went into the police station. "I'm trying to get an address for a friend," Nancy explained to the chunky desk sergeant who asked to help them. "There was a girl in town a while back named Diana Spitzer. She left something at my friend's house, and we lost her address. Do you think you'd have anything in your files?"

"Only if she's got a criminal record," the sergeant joked. Then he became serious. "Who's your friend?" he asked. "I can't give out that kind of information to just anyone."

"Eloise Drew, she's—" Nancy began.

The sergeant's face cleared. "I've met her," he said. "She's a friend of Vivienne Worthington."

"Right." Nancy nodded. "She's staying at Mrs. Worthington's house this summer."

"Nice lady, Ms. Drew. She knows my wife. Let me see what I can do."

Nancy and Bess sat on the bench and waited. After a while the sergeant returned with a file in his hand.

"You know, I just remembered," he said conversationally, "Ms. Drew has a niece she's always bragging about. She's a detective. You wouldn't know her, would you?"

Nancy blushed. "You caught me," she admitted. "I'm Nancy Drew." She stuck out her hand.

"Thought so. I'm Larry Jones," he said, shaking her hand firmly. "Ms. Drew says you're famous."

"She sure is!" Bess piped up loyally, then introduced herself.

"Well, your Diana isn't a criminal," Sergeant Jones said cheerfully, opening his file. "But she did get a parking ticket while she was here. Here's an address in Manhattan."

"That's perfect. Thank you very much!" Nancy said gratefully. Then a thought struck her. "There's another thing. I wonder if the officer who investigated Nicholas Scott's death is here? I called a couple of days ago and was told he might be back today."

"That's me," he answered, surprised. "Why?"

"I was curious about the circumstances," Nancy replied. "Do you mind if I talk to you for a minute?"

Sergeant Jones gave Nancy a long look. "Sure," he said at last. "Come back to my desk. You're on a case, aren't you? Next thing I know, you'll be asking to see police files!"

"As a matter of fact," Nancy replied pleasantly, "I was about to do just that."

Sergeant Jones frowned. "What on earth for?"

"Well," Nancy said slowly, "I have reason to

believe Nicholas Scott's death may have been murder."

To Nancy's chagrin, he burst out laughing. "Murder? Are you kidding? We know it was an accident beyond a shadow of a doubt. I have an eyewitness!"

Chapter

Twelve

AN EYEWITNESS in the middle of the night?"
Nancy asked doubtfully.

"Sure, night fishing is pretty common around
here," Sergeant Jones replied. "One of the
local fishermen talked to him on the radio. As a
matter of fact, he told Nicholas he was going in
because of the weather and advised him to do
the same. Nicholas refused, so Tony—that's the
fisherman—headed over toward him to keep an
eye on him."

"Did he see the accident?"

"Enough of it. Visibility wasn't great. Seems
Nicholas's boat hit the rocks and broke up. He
hit his head as he was knocked overboard. Tony
got there as fast as he could, but it was too late.

111

"Sorry," the sergeant said, seeing Nancy's disappointed face. "The injuries were consistent with Tony's story. And we checked for foreign substances. No drugs, no alcohol."

"Well, I certainly feel silly," Nancy said, apologizing. "I'm sorry I wasted your time."

"No problem," Sergeant Jones replied. "Anything to help out a famous detective. Better luck next time!"

So Nicholas Scott wasn't murdered, Nancy thought as she and Bess headed home. The message Nancy had received at the Lobster Tank had sent her in the wrong direction. Did that mean the second message, warning her away from the *Vanity* and Diana Spitzer, had been meant to mislead her, too? Maybe the painting wasn't important to the case after all.

It was possible, she reasoned, but the red-haired model *did* come all the way out to the Hamptons to buy the painting. She must want it for some reason, and Nancy was going to have to lure her back to town to find out why.

Using the address she got at the police station, Nancy got a telephone number for Diana Spitzer in Manhattan. The girl answered on the first ring.

"Is this Diana Spitzer?" Nancy asked from her aunt's house.

"Yes, who's this?"

"A friend from the Hamptons," Nancy replied. "I heard you were back in town to buy your painting."

The girl on the other end of the line gasped. "Who *is* this?" she asked, her voice high and tense. "Did Bob put you up to this?"

So Bob Tercero *was* involved! Nancy thought. "I'm a friend, and I have what you want," she said, being deliberately vague. "Can you meet me in the town square tomorrow?"

"I—I guess," the girl said slowly. "Do you have my hairpin, too?"

"We'll talk tomorrow," Nancy promised. "Tomorrow at six o'clock."

"How will I recognize you?" Diana asked.

"Don't worry, I'll recognize you," Nancy said. She hung up before the other girl could reply.

"What did she say?" Bess asked.

"She asked if Bob put me up to this," Nancy told her. "She was scared stiff. And then she asked me if I had her hairpin."

"Her hairpin!" Bess snorted. "What a time to be thinking about fashion!"

Nancy shook her head. "It's something else. When Diana asked Cynthia about the painting she mentioned the hairpin, too. It must be important to her for some reason."

"Incriminating evidence?" Bess suggested.

"But of what?" Nancy asked, troubled.

The two girls headed for the Nisus Gallery to meet Doug Coggins.

"I don't understand how Doug is going to help us find Christopher," Bess said as they drove.

"Actually," Nancy said slowly, "I'm beginning

to wonder whether we're going to find him at all."

"What?" Bess asked, alarmed.

"No one but Nicholas had seen Christopher in the last six months," Nancy explained. "That was just after Bob said Christopher finished the *Vanity.*"

"Yes," Bess said. "Go on."

"The point is, we have only Bob's word that Nicholas saw Christopher in the past six months. Megan practically lived in the studio, and she never even met the man. Now *that's* weird.

"Then there's Christopher's behavior. According to one critic, Christopher's work has been going downhill recently. And he didn't show up for his nephew's funeral. You'd think that he'd have come since, according to Bob, they were so devoted to each other."

"I don't see the connection," Bess said, frowning.

"There's not much of one," Nancy admitted. "But there is the *Vanity.* Is it only coincidence that all Christopher's paintings since that one have been mediocre? Or that Diana Spitzer suddenly reappeared after the rumors of Christopher's disappearance and Nicholas's tragic accident?"

"But Nicholas's death *was* an accident," Bess said.

"It looks that way."

"What do you mean, 'looks that way'?" Bess demanded. She sounded exasperated. "There was an eyewitness, Nan! How much more evidence do you need?"

Nancy massaged the bridge of her nose with her fingers. "I know you're right. But I also know there's something I'm not seeing—something to do with Nicholas and Christopher and painting. Something that's right in front of my eyes."

Something else was bothering Nancy. When she'd studied the accounts at the Nisus Gallery, she'd been hunting for the *Vanity.* She hadn't looked back any farther. The accounts in Christopher's name were consistent after the painting was done but maybe not before. She resolved to check the ledgers again when she got there.

Doug Coggins was waiting on the porch in front of the gallery when the girls arrived.

"Now, just what am I looking for?" Doug asked inside.

"Forgery," Nancy replied in a low voice. "I have reason to believe that a painting attributed to Christopher Scott was painted by someone else. I thought you could check some of his work here to see whether it looks right to you."

Doug shrugged. "They looked fine to me the last two times I was here, but I didn't study them." He walked over to the large pink canvas. "It should be easy to determine. Chris's brush strokes are very distinctive, and he mixes all his own colors."

Doug examined the painting, frowning as he

concentrated. Nancy and Bess waited anxiously.

Doug leaned forward, squinting at a small square of the painting. His frown deepened.

Suddenly he turned around and stared at Nancy. "You're right," he said. "This is not the work of Christopher Scott!"

Chapter

Thirteen

ARE YOU SURE?" Nancy asked.

Doug nodded vigorously. "Christopher never used a premixed color; he always added a tinge of something else. Look here," he said, pointing to a corner of the canvas. "This is definitely a stock pink."

Doug leaned closer to the painting. "Now this area," he began, then hesitated, *"does* look like Christopher's work. In fact, look at the brush strokes. It has to be his!"

The two girls exchanged glances.

"So you're not sure?" Bess asked.

Doug crinkled his nose and stood back from the canvas. "I'm a little confused," he admitted. "This section looks like his, and that one doesn't.

The painting as a whole is kind of mixed-up. But no one could forge those brush strokes. It may be that Christopher was experimenting with a new style."

Nancy wasn't so sure. Doug's evaluation of the painting supported a theory growing in her mind.

"Would you say that it looks like Christopher Scott painted *parts* of this painting?" she asked Doug.

"Parts? I don't think Christopher would ever let anyone help him with a painting. He's too vain."

After thanking the painter for his help, Nancy asked Cecilia if either Bob or Cynthia was around. She was told that Bob had the day off, but Cynthia was due back any minute.

"I'm going with Doug to his studio, Nancy," Bess informed her friend. "We're going to work on that painting of me."

"I'll see you later, then. Will you be back for our rendezvous with Diana this evening?"

"You bet!" Bess said. "I'll see you back at the house at about four-thirty or five."

Nancy asked Cecilia for permission to use the phone in Bob Tercero's office. After slipping inside, she locked the door and went straight for the book of checks. This time she looked back to the payments issued a year ago.

It was just as she'd suspected, she noted with satisfaction. Christopher Scott's payments varied in size. Sometimes they were only ten thousand dollars, but in one case, the artist had been paid forty thousand dollars! She looked for a pattern over the past several years. Even though they varied, the payments grew in size. Because, Nancy was sure, of the artist's growing reputation.

Then, six months ago, the payments changed form. Scott started getting a straight fifteen thousand dollars for every painting. Did Christopher request this? she wondered. Or was there another, more sinister reason? Her eyes narrowing thoughtfully, Nancy closed the book.

"Nancy?" Cynthia Gray inquired through the closed door. She tried the handle. "Why is the door locked? Are you okay in there?"

Nancy leapt up and opened the door.

"Cecilia said you needed to make a phone call," Cynthia said suspiciously, entering the room. "She said you've been in here for a while."

Nancy took a deep breath. "You'd better sit down," she told the gallery owner. "I have something to say that might interest you.

"What do you know about ART Inc.?" Nancy asked, after Cynthia had taken a seat by Bob's desk.

From the expression on Cynthia's face, it was clear she had never even heard of the company. Using the account books, Nancy explained that she had discovered Bob was stealing from the gallery by selling paintings to himself at reduced rates.

"I can't believe it!" Cynthia said when Nancy had finished. "I trusted Bob with everything! It's not even the fact that he was stealing from the gallery that bothers me as much as that he was cheating our artists." Cynthia paused. "But why on earth were you looking at our accounts?"

"There's something fishy about Christopher Scott's work over the last six months or so," Nancy replied. "I was hoping I could find something in your payments to explain it."

"And did you?"

"Possibly," Nancy said. "Since February all your payments to Christopher Scott have been exactly fifteen thousand dollars. Does that seem likely to you?"

"Usually the price of a painting depends on its size and other factors," Cynthia said slowly. "And by now, I'd think Chris would be getting more than that for each painting. Does this have anything to do with ART?"

"It doesn't seem to," Nancy admitted. "But it could have something to do with Christopher's disappearance. I'm wondering whether the change in payments means that Bob has some hold over him. Or maybe Bob just decided that Scott's work wasn't worth any more than that. In that case, maybe Christopher was unhappy with the drop in his payments and decided to go to a new gallery."

"If Bob was blackmailing Chris, why pay him at all?" Cynthia asked. She still sounded furious. "Or why not sell *his* paintings to ART? Bob was obviously paying Christopher something, because all the checks are made out to him."

"I don't know, but there's a trail of money here, and I'm going to follow it. Do you know where Bob keeps canceled checks?" Nancy asked.

Cynthia shook her head regretfully. "I really never paid any attention to the way Bob ran my business. I'm beginning to see what a mistake that was."

Together Nancy and Cynthia flipped through Bob's files for old checks but with no success. After a few minutes Cynthia snapped her fingers.

"You know, there's an easier way to go about this. I know which bank Christopher uses," Cynthia offered. "And one of the managers there is a friend of mine. Her name is Ann James. If I called her, I'm sure she'd help."

"That'd be great," Nancy said. "Thank you."

"Thank *you*," Cynthia returned. "When I see that rat Bob Tercero, I'm not only going to fire him, I'm going to press charges!"

With a decided nod, Cynthia picked up the phone and called the bank.

"Ann, how are you? I wonder if you could do me a huge favor?

"There's a young woman here I'd like you to talk to," she continued, after getting a favorable response. "Her name is Nancy Drew, and she's conducting a sort of investigation into Christopher Scott's affairs. I'm all mixed up in it, I'm afraid; it has to do with Nisus's payments to him."

Cynthia thanked Ann and turned the telephone over to Nancy.

Nancy checked with the bank manager to make sure that all the gallery's payments had indeed been deposited into Scott's bank account. They had, but she had expected that. It would be too easy for an investigator to discover any discrepancies if the payments had not been made to that account.

"Can you check withdrawals?" Nancy asked the bank manager. "I am especially interested in the month of February, and also any activity from two weeks ago. Are there any large withdrawals?"

Nancy could hear computer keys clicking as Ann looked up her information. "Nothing large or unusual since February, really," Ann said at last. "And nothing at all in the last few weeks."

Nothing? Nancy thought hard for a minute. "I'm sorry, but could we go back to the payments, then? Is there any way to check whether Christopher endorsed the checks himself?"

"Not from here," Ann said, "but if Cynthia has the canceled checks, she could look for you."

"Yes, we thought of that," Nancy said with a frustrated sigh. "I guess we'll have to keep searching for them."

"But remember," Ann cautioned, "even if he didn't sign them, it probably doesn't mean anything. We don't require an endorsing signature if the check is made out to the person who holds the account. All we need is the account number on the back of the check."

Nancy was frustrated. "Is there anything else?" she asked. "Anything that's unusual at all?"

"Well, there is one thing, but it's not *unusual*," Ann began, "and I guess it doesn't really matter anymore."

"What is it?" Nancy asked quickly. "At this point, anything would help."

"As I said, it won't help you now because Nicholas is dead," the bank manager said. "But while he was alive, Nicholas had power of attorney over his uncle's accounts."

Chapter

Fourteen

NANCY DREW IN her breath. So Nicholas had unlimited access to his uncle's money! "Can you find out how often Nicholas withdrew money from the account?" she asked.

"Not with automated teller machines," Ann said. "Anyone with a card can take money out at any time. There's no way of knowing which withdrawals were made by Nicholas and which by Christopher."

Nancy thanked her for all her help and hung up. "That about wraps it up," she told Cynthia. "I think I know what's going on. I don't have time to explain now, but I'll let you know how it turns out!"

Nancy raced home. As she hurried in the door, she heard the phone ringing.

"Nancy, is that you?" George poked her head out of the kitchen doorway, her eyes wide. "You have a telephone call."

Nancy reached over the kitchen counter and picked up the phone. "Hello?" she said breathlessly. Whoever it was, Nancy would have to call back later. She had a lot to do this afternoon!

"Hello, yourself," Ned Nickerson's voice greeted her warmly. "How's my favorite girl?"

"Ned!" Nancy's heart leapt. "How are you? I haven't heard from you in ages!"

"Well, that's about to change because I have a plane ticket in my hand that will get me to the Hamptons in two weeks."

"A plane ticket?" Nancy repeated. Ned was coming in two weeks? She sat down abruptly as she realized what that meant. What on earth was she going to do about Sasha?

"Well, don't sound so excited. Is there a problem?" Ned asked. His voice was a little hesitant.

Now she'd hurt his feelings! "No, no problem," Nancy said forcefully. "It'll be great to see you."

"It doesn't sound that way," Ned said. "What's wrong, Nan?"

The concern in his voice made Nancy realize how much she loved him. "Nothing's wrong," she said. "I'm just in the middle of a mystery, that's all."

"Oh, no." Ned groaned playfully. "Then I'll never see you! Forget it, I won't come."

"No, please come. I'll be done by then," Nancy promised.

"You know I was only kidding. You couldn't keep me away if you tried," Ned said cheerfully. "I really miss you, Nan."

"I miss you, too," Nancy replied, her eyes filling with tears.

"Nancy, are you okay?" The worry crept back into Ned's voice. "You sound like you're going to cry."

"Of course I'm okay," she insisted. "I just love you, that's all."

"That's all?" Ned asked. "That's a lot. I love you, too, Nan. I'm sorry I haven't been able to come see you sooner."

"It's all right. I know you'd be here if I needed you."

"I won't let anything stop me this time," he vowed.

When Nancy hung up the phone, she was shaking. "You guys can come in now," she called to Bess and George, who were hovering in the hall.

"We weren't eavesdropping," Bess said defensively as the cousins settled themselves around the kitchen table.

"Really, we weren't," George put in. "We were just, um, nearby."

"Well, you heard it anyway," Nancy said. "What do I do now?"

"What do you want to do?" Bess asked.

"I don't know!" Nancy sank into a chair. "Sasha is so romantic, and when I'm with him, well, I guess I can forget everything, including Ned. Does that sound horrible?"

"Not at all," Bess said. "This has been a summer full of romance."

"But when I heard Ned's voice, it was like . . . like being *home* somehow. I don't know how to describe it. I really do miss him."

"It's a tough one," George agreed. "They're both great guys. I guess you have to go with your heart."

Bess glared at her cousin. "Honestly, George, that's the problem!" Bess exclaimed. "She doesn't know where that is!"

"She'll know," George said simply. "When she can see both of them together."

"I hope so," Nancy said, "because I sure don't know right now."

The three girls sank into silence.

"What time is it?" Nancy asked suddenly.

"Just after five," George answered.

"I'd better get moving. Are you guys ready to meet our mysterious model?"

"So soon?" Bess asked. "I thought you said six."

"I did. But I want to stop at the gallery first."

"How's it coming?" George asked. "I feel like I've missed most of what's been going on."

Nancy filled her in. "The key is in the paintings," she said. "But it looks like Diana Spitzer is the only one who can confirm everything. There's one more thing I have to check out with Cynthia Gray."

"What's that?" George asked.

"Something I overheard at the opening party for the Scott show," Nancy said mysteriously.

"Nancy!" Bess wailed.

"Okay, okay." Nancy threw up her hands. "I need her opinion on whether Christopher Scott's painting has changed over the past six months. How do you like that for an answer?"

"No good," George declared. "Tell us the rest."

"I can't until I talk to Diana. All I have now are vague ideas," Nancy said. "We'll find out the truth together."

Bess and George offered to go with Nancy to the Nisus Gallery, but she refused, saying it was only a quick question and she didn't want to stay too long. The three girls drove into town and Nancy dropped Bess and George off at Bess's favorite boutique. They made plans to meet at the town square a little before six to confront the model together.

"Don't go near her till I get there," Nancy warned as she said goodbye to them. "If I'm right, she may spook easily."

When Nancy got to the gallery, she found the place dark and the front door ajar. That's odd, she thought uneasily. The gallery was usually open until six. And if it had closed early, why hadn't someone locked up?

"Hello? Cynthia?" Nancy called. She turned on the light switch and walked in. "Anyone here?"

Nancy walked down the hall to Cynthia's office and tapped on the door. "Cynthia?" Nancy pulled open the door, which swung out into the hall.

Just then Bob Tercero's door flew open. "Well, if it isn't our little detective!" Bob said sarcastically, trapping Nancy between him and the open door. "Here to stir up more trouble?

"Stay right where you are," he warned as Nancy tried to step around him. "I've been fired, so I don't have any reason to be nice to you anymore."

"You've only been fired," Nancy said defiantly, "not arrested, so it looks to me like you got off easy. You won't be so lucky if you try to stop me from leaving."

Bob just grinned. "Look at her," he said to no one in particular. "A little girl playing detective. But you found the wrong things. You couldn't figure out what happened to Christopher even when I handed you the clues!"

"Is that what you think?" Nancy asked angrily. "It might interest you to know I found the *Vanity*. Someone stole it before you could!"

Bob's face darkened. "Where is it?"

Nancy returned his stare. "I don't have it."

"I'm warning you," Bob said, advancing on her. "I'll use force." He grabbed her arm, twisting it behind her back. "Now tell me who has it."

"You're hurting me!" Nancy cried, stalling for time. How was she going to get out of the gallery? she thought wildly.

"Okay, okay," she gasped. "I'll tell you if you just let me go."

Bob released her arm, shoving her into Cynthia's office. He closed the door.

"Put your hands on your head and sit on the floor, your back up against the wall," he directed. "Stretch your legs flat out in front of you."

Nancy obeyed slowly. She thought she had a good chance of beating him if it came to a struggle, but she decided not to risk it if she didn't have to. If she just did what he said, maybe she could defuse the situation before anyone got hurt.

"Now tell me who has the painting," Bob said.

"Diana Spitzer has it, of course," Nancy lied. "Who else? I sent her into hiding."

"So, Diana's back? She would have been a lot better off if she'd stayed away."

"Well, Nancy," Bob said with contempt, "you were right and I was wrong. You *do* know too much." He picked up the small bronze statue Cynthia had placed on a pedestal near the door. "You didn't take my warning seriously. I think it's time I got serious about removing you from the scene."

Bob advanced on her. Nancy tried to rise, but

he was too fast for her. One arm snaked out and pushed her back to the floor.

Bob lunged at her, the statue raised above his head. She rolled away, but the blow still caught the side of her head.

"That's for lying," Nancy heard Bob say just before she blacked out.

Chapter

Fifteen

THROUGH A HAZE Nancy heard someone talking.

"Nancy? Wake up." Nancy felt something caress her face. "Please wake up."

Ned? Nancy thought groggily. Was Ned here? The voice was deep and tender, like his. But the accent was different. . . . Nancy forced her eyes to open.

Sasha's face swam before her eyes.

"Sasha? What are you doing here?" she mumbled. Her tongue felt too big for her mouth.

"Nancy, you are all right!" Sasha burst out, worry easing from his face. "I thought you were dead."

Nancy sat up, wincing in pain. She put her hand to her temple and groaned. "What's going on? What time is it?"

"It is six o'clock," Sasha said, cradling Nancy against him. "I ran into Bess and George on the street. They were worried when you did not show up. I offered to come here to look for you. Bess was going to call Tommy to meet them at the town square. She and George seemed to think they might need someone with a car."

"The town square!" Nancy said, pulling herself forward. "Sasha, we've got to get to Diana."

"No way!" Sasha declared. "You are in no shape to go anywhere."

"We have to," Nancy insisted. "Bob Tercero was here, and now Diana Spitzer is in danger. I told him she has the *Vanity* painting. He's desperate. If he sees her in town, who knows what he'll do!"

Nancy struggled to her feet with Sasha hovering anxiously over her. "I'll be okay," she assured him, one hand on her head. "Could you find my purse? I've got some aspirin in it."

Sasha brought the aspirin and some water from the bathroom. "Thanks," Nancy said gratefully, gulping it down. "Now call the police. Tell them to arrest Bob Tercero. I'll go sit in the car."

"What should I say are the charges?"

"Anything and everything!" Nancy replied. "Thievery, assault—and let's just hope that's all."

"Nancy," he protested as he headed for the phone, "wait for the police. You are in no condition to drive."

"I'll be okay," Nancy repeated, gritting her teeth as her head throbbed. "Anyway, we don't have any choice."

Nancy waited in the car, massaging her temples gently. Bob Tercero had said, "That's for lying," she recalled. What did he mean? She watched as Sasha stepped out of the gallery and closed the door behind him. Well, she thought, when the police picked Bob up, she'd have plenty of time to ask him about his cryptic remark.

Nancy drove to the town square as fast as her pounding head would allow. As they pulled up, George raced up to the car.

"She's gone," George said, leaning down to the window on the driver's side. "You said not to approach her, so Bess and Tommy followed her in Tommy's car." She looked at Nancy. "What on earth happened to you?"

"I had a 'conversation' with Bob Tercero," Nancy said, touching her head lightly. "But I ducked. I think I'm okay."

George knew better than to argue. "Whatever you say. I'll drive if you don't feel up to it.

"Bess said she'd call the house as soon as she knows where Diana is headed," George explained, opening the driver's side door. Sasha climbed into the backseat, and Nancy slid over to the passenger side gratefully. "Eloise is home manning the phones," George added.

"I'll call your aunt to see if Bess has checked in yet," Sasha volunteered. "Just pull over to that pay phone."

While Sasha was gone, Nancy told George what had happened. "We called the police, so they'll be on the lookout for Bob," she concluded.

Sasha returned. "Bess did call," he said, climbing in and slamming the car door. "Diana stopped at the gallery, and now she is heading toward New York City. She's in a white Volvo sedan. I wrote down her license plate number."

"Bravo for Bess!" Nancy declared. "Can we catch up with them?"

George gunned the engine. The little car raced through the narrow streets. They passed the gallery and headed out of town. The asphalt road got straighter and wider. "George, I hope you're not breaking any speed laws," Nancy said to her friend.

George raised her eyebrows. "Not yet, but I will be if I keep accelerating," she replied.

George caught up with Bess and Tommy several miles out of town. She pulled into the left lane beside Tommy's car. Bess waved and pointed forward. George pulled ahead.

Thank goodness there were no other cars on the road, Nancy thought. They were racing down a wide straightaway, heading for the next town.

A few minutes later the back of a white Volvo appeared in the distance. "We've got to stop her," Nancy urged. "I have to talk to her before Bob Tercero finds her."

George put her foot down hard on the gas pedal. "Hang on. I hope there are no police cars around!"

As they drew up behind Diana's car, the white Volvo took off in front of them.

"Some people just do not want help, do they?" Sasha said in disgust.

"She's scared," Nancy said. "She doesn't know we're friends."

"Well, she's not going to know unless she stops," George declared. "I can keep up with her, but I'm not going to force her off the road!"

The two cars raced along the road at high speed, George right on Diana's tail. Tommy and Bess were no longer in sight. Slow down, Diana, slow down! Nancy pleaded silently.

Houses began appearing along the road. In front of them, Nancy could see the edge of the next town.

"Watch out, George," she warned.

Suddenly Diana's car slowed. George slammed on her brakes to avoid ramming the Volvo. Both cars pulled off to the side of the road in front of a house.

Diana leapt out of the Volvo and ran for the house. Sasha and George jumped out after her.

"Wait!" Sasha called.

Diana looked behind her and ran faster, but Sasha and George were closing in. Nancy, her head throbbing, tried to keep up.

Sasha reached Diana and grabbed her arm. She stumbled, and the two of them rolled together on the lawn. Nancy followed, wincing in pain.

Diana sat up and looked at Sasha, a terrified expression on her face.

"I'm leaving," she said in a small voice. "I promise I'll never tell. Please don't kill me, too!"

Chapter

Sixteen

WHEN SHE HEARD Diana's desperate words, Nancy's suspicions were confirmed. Feeling satisfied, she knelt by the redheaded model. "Don't worry, we aren't going to hurt you," she assured Diana.

At that moment Tommy and Bess pulled up.

"Everything's fine," Nancy called across the lawn, waving to them to stay where they were. She turned back to Diana. "I think we'd better move. We can go sit in Tommy's car and talk if that's all right with you?"

"Are you the one who called me?" Diana gasped, not moving.

Nancy nodded.

"Then you're a friend of Bob's!"

"A friend!" Sasha snorted angrily. "Some friend. Look what he gave her!" Sasha tilted Nancy's head so Diana could see the bruise on her temple.

Diana's eyes widened. She stood up and started to move toward Tommy's car.

"What did you mean, 'don't kill me, too'?" George asked Diana. "Nicholas Scott *was* murdered, then?"

Diana didn't answer, but Nancy shook her head. "Not Nicholas, I'm afraid. It was Christopher Scott who was murdered."

George and Sasha looked stunned. "What are you saying?" Sasha asked as they climbed into Tommy's jeep.

"It's the only thing that makes sense. It was the comments I heard about Christopher's work deteriorating and about there being no unfinished paintings of his lying around that clinched it for me," Nancy explained. "But maybe we should let Diana tell it." She smiled encouragingly at the red-haired girl.

Diana glanced around uneasily. "Who *are* you?" she asked, bewildered. "And how do you know so much?"

"Nancy's a detective," George said, nodding at her. "She was asked by Cynthia Gray to find Christopher Scott. But from what you seem to be saying, she came onto the scene a little too late."

Diana nodded. "I met Nicholas at a nightclub

last fall," she began. "We started dating casually, and he introduced me to Christopher. Christopher wanted to paint my portrait.

"Christopher was wonderful to me. He was very fatherly. We liked each other immediately. He paints very slowly, so the portrait was taking a long time. We spent most of our days together.

"Nicholas was jealous. There wasn't anything romantic between me and Chris, but Nick couldn't see that. After a while he decided he didn't want me to sit for Chris anymore. He was very unhappy about it. He ordered me to stop, and the two of them fought about it.

"I don't know if you ever met Nick, but he was pretty wild," Diana continued, twisting her hands.

Nancy nodded. "We've heard something like that," she murmured. "Apparently he wasn't too popular."

"He was awful," Diana said simply. "He could be incredibly charming, but all he really cared about was himself. He and Chris quarreled constantly about money, but Chris always gave in and Nicholas got what he wanted.

"On the night the painting was finished, Chris and I planned to celebrate." Diana stopped, her eyes filling with tears. "Chris was about to open a bottle of champagne when Nicholas walked in.

"He brought Bob Tercero with him, to see the painting, I guess. He picked up the hairpin from the table—you've seen it in the portrait, haven't you?"

"I haven't," Sasha said.

Diana shuddered. "It's about twelve inches long, and pointed. It looks like a silver chopstick with a sharp end. Nicholas sat and toyed with it, rolling it over and over in his hands as he ordered me to get dressed so we could go out dancing. He was furious that I had been celebrating without him."

Diana looked at Nancy pleadingly. "Well, Chris didn't like it, and they fought—again. But this time it was terrible. I didn't want to go out with Nicholas after the way he'd treated Chris, and I said so. Nicholas flew into a rage and blamed Chris because I wouldn't go with him. He launched himself at Chris and they began to struggle. My hairpin was still in Nick's hand. And somehow he stabbed Chris. I don't think Nicholas meant to kill him." Diana shuddered.

"Wow," George murmured. Nancy patted Diana's shoulder, encouraging her to go on with her story.

"When Nicholas saw what he had done, he panicked," Diana said. "That was when Bob took over. He told Nick to take the body out in one of the boats and sink it. Then, when Nick was gone, Bob made me promise never to tell. He said if I did he and Nick would swear *I* had done it. He said the painting and my hairpin would be all the 'evidence' he needed."

Nancy thought she could guess the rest. "With Christopher dead," she put in, "Nicholas had no money. But there were a lot of unfinished paintings around.

"Nicholas could paint a little, something that not many people knew. Of course, he wasn't the genius Christopher was, but he could do a fair imitation of his uncle's style if he had something to start with. So he began finishing the stuff Christopher had left undone, and Bob sold the forgeries. They must have split the money they made on the paintings. There was no reason for anyone to be suspicious—no one ever saw Christopher around anyway. If he was still turning out paintings, no one would ever suspect he was dead.

"But I guess Nicholas felt guilty. I think he must have really cared about Christopher, or else Christopher wouldn't have been so devoted to him. Anyway, Megan Archer said Nicholas had mood swings. He often escaped to his boat. He was running out of paintings to finish, and he was worried about that.

"That's why Megan's description of him is so different from everyone else's," Nancy continued. "I kept thinking it was love that made her see him differently, but then I realized that couldn't be the only reason. Even love isn't that blind—Nicholas must have really changed. He must have been feeling guilty and getting scared about what would happen when there were no paintings left to finish."

Diana picked up the story. "I wanted to buy the *Vanity* and destroy it, but it was never exhibited. When I heard Nicholas was dead, I thought I'd come back and look for it. That way, there would be no proof that I was there that night with the murder weapon in my hand." She grimaced. "But I guess Bob Tercero has the painting hidden somewhere—and he'll hold it over me as a threat for the rest of my life."

"Don't worry about Bob," Nancy reassured her. "He's got a lot to answer for—the police should be picking him up any minute on charges of assaulting me. And the painting is safe with Nicholas's girlfriend, Megan."

"I guess I should go to the police, too," Diana said in a dull voice. "I really am responsible. I helped cover up a murder."

"That's true," Nancy admitted, "but I don't think they'll be too hard on you. After all, you're the only witness."

Diana shook her head. "It'll be my word against Bob's."

"Well, let's stop by Megan's house and pick up the *Vanity,* then," Nancy suggested. "And I'll go with you to the police station."

Nancy joined Diana in the white Volvo, so that she could go over all the details of the case with the girl.

Tommy and Bess led the way back through town, past the Scotts' estate, to Megan's house. When the three cars pulled into the driveway, Megan's house was a blaze of light in the deepening dusk. Nancy looked over toward the Scotts' boat house, silhouetted against the setting sun.

They trooped up the front steps, Nancy in the lead.

"Don't worry," Nancy told Diana, seeing her uneasy expression. "I'm sure Megan will lend us the painting when she hears why we need it."

The door opened partway very slowly. Megan's face appeared strained.

"Nancy," she began.

The door flew all the way open, and a man leapt at Nancy. He spun her around and grabbed her by the throat.

It was Bob Tercero, and he was holding something against Nancy's back.

"Stop right there," he warned the startled crowd. "I have a gun, and I promise you I'll use it!"

Chapter

Seventeen

Everybody inside," Bob ordered, dragging Nancy with him. "I want all of you on the couch where I can see you."

Out of the corner of her eye, Nancy saw the *Vanity* painting propped against the wall next to the sliding glass doors. Bob shoved her just then, so she lost her balance and fell forward onto the couch. Sasha caught her arm and steadied her, giving it a reassuring squeeze.

"What a pleasure!" Bob crowed, waving his gun at the huddled group. "Two redheaded meddlers in one room. I see you didn't heed my warning about lying," he said to Nancy.

"What are you talking about?" Nancy asked, trying to sound calm.

"You lied about the painting. That was dumb," he growled. "There was never any way Diana could have taken it. Nicholas *did* die in an accident, you see. It wasn't planned, so Diana couldn't have known about it and gotten to the painting before me."

"How did you know to come here?" Nancy asked.

"I always thought Nicholas had hidden it," Bob admitted, "but then you told me someone had taken it before I could. Megan was the only answer."

So that's what he had meant! Nancy had slipped and put everyone in danger. She could have kicked herself.

"Why come to get it?" she asked. "You had a head start to safety. Why not just get away?"

"The *Vanity* is Christopher Scott's only portrait and his last real painting," Bob replied. "When the word gets out that Nick forged the others, this one will be priceless."

"Well, the priceless painting won't do you any good in jail," Nancy said. "Look around you, Bob. There are seven of us here. How do you think you're going to get away?"

Bob laughed. "You're an awfully cocky girl," he said. *"I'm* the one with the gun."

Sasha looked at Tommy, and both guys stood up.

"Watch yourselves," Bob said, waving the gun back and forth. "I'll shoot."

But Nancy could tell Bob was scared. "I *will*

shoot!" he repeated. He backed toward the glass doors, the gun pointed at Nancy. She stood up and took a step toward him.

"Get away from me," he shouted. Then he fired the gun at the ceiling.

Diana screamed.

"Watch out!" Nancy cried, ducking. "Everybody, hit the floor!"

George grabbed Megan, who had started to cry. "Is everyone okay?" she asked. "Megan, were you hit?"

Megan shook her head. "Just shaken."

"Where's Bob?" Tommy asked, one arm around a shaking Bess.

The glass doors were open and the painting was gone. Bob had escaped!

The young people poured out the doorway and onto the lawn. Nancy heard the roar of a powerboat engine being started. "The dock!" she cried. "He's taking one of Nicholas's boats!"

Nancy, George, and the guys took off for the Scotts' studio, the other girls right behind them. Nancy was right—Nicholas's boat was headed in the direction of town.

"Jump in the other one!" Tommy called, his feet pounding the wooden dock. He leapt into the boat and pulled the cord on the engine. It sputtered to life.

"Let's go," Nancy directed as George and Sasha climbed in, too. She waved to Diana and Bess. "Stay here," she yelled. "Call the police."

Tommy steered toward Tercero's boat. "Everyone to the stern," Tommy shouted over the engine. "We'll go faster that way."

"Can we catch him?" George asked anxiously.

"I don't know," Tommy admitted. "But he's pretty far out, and he'll have to come back in to dock—if he's going to town. If we stay close to shore, we ought to make up some time."

The wind whipped Nancy's hair around her face, and she had to squint to see Bob's boat in the deepening dusk. "Is he turning in toward land yet?" she shouted to Tommy.

"Looks like it. There's a dock nearby. He must be heading for it."

Nancy and her friends were slowly gaining on Bob. "I think we're going to make it," she said, pointing toward the shore. "There's the dock."

Bob was trying to maneuver the boat beside the long wooden dock sticking out in front of the town's main marina. There were sailboats and luxury boats of all sizes tied up in rows in neighboring slips.

"We're in luck," Tommy said happily. "He doesn't know how to steer it in. At this rate he's going to crash right into the pier."

Tommy cut the engine. "Sasha, take this rope and get on the bow. Hold on to the cleat so you don't fall off. When I get close, jump onto the dock and tie us up."

Bob had made it to the dock without mishap and was trying to climb out of the boat. "He's getting away!" George warned.

"Jump now!" Tommy yelled.

Sasha jumped, throwing the looped end of the rope around the cleat on the dock. The dancer landed on the dock five feet from Bob Tercero. Bob spun around—and pointed the gun at Sasha!

"Look out!" Nancy cried.

Sasha rolled and did a handspring. His right leg shot out, karate-style, and kicked Bob's gun neatly out of the way. It clattered along the dock. Bob roared in fury and threw a punch. Nancy watched anxiously as the two fought. Sasha threw his shoulder into Bob's chest, knocking the man off balance. Then, to Nancy's horror, Sasha grabbed at his left arm and stumbled backward.

"His shoulder!" she gasped, remembering Sasha's spill when they had gone waterskiing. He must have reinjured it. Bob, seeing his advantage, ran for the gun.

"Sasha, be careful!" Nancy screamed. She scrambled onto the dock and launched herself at Tercero. Her body hit his, and then they were airborne, flying off the dock. Nancy stubbornly held on to Bob's waist as they hit the water.

Keep him off balance, Nancy told herself. She grabbed his head, trying to force him underwater. His hands reached up for her, pulling her under with him. She gulped air quickly, struggling to get free.

Nancy held her breath. Tercero was stronger, but she had caught him off guard, and he hadn't taken a deep breath before going under. Now she had to keep that advantage. She grabbed his arm

149

firmly and dove for the bottom. She had to keep him under until his air ran out.

Bob dropped his hold on Nancy, the air from his lungs bubbling toward the surface in a cloud. She had him! Nancy tightened her hold. She counted to ten and then let him go, kicking quickly up behind him. She dragged his choking body back to the dock and turned him over to Tommy, who hoisted him up.

Nancy dropped down on the dock next to Sasha. "I didn't know you knew karate," she said weakly. She could hear police sirens in the distance.

"I don't—I just picked that move up from watching American TV," Sasha confessed.

Nancy stared at him. He had taken an awful risk. "Good thing it worked," she said at last.

"Good thing you can hold your breath for so long," he countered, hugging her tightly.

Nancy spent the rest of the night with Diana at the police station, and they made their statements. The next day she slept late, and in the afternoon Nancy accompanied Sergeant Jones to the site of Nicholas's accident. If she was right, the other old wreck she'd seen down there held some crucial answers. But this time, she stayed in the boat when the divers went down.

By the time Nancy got back to her aunt Eloise's house, she was exhausted.

"Thank goodness you're home," Eloise said as Nancy walked in the door. She was sitting in the living room with Bess and George. "Bess was worried. She kept saying, 'But Nancy's going to miss the bonfire.'"

"A bonfire!" Nancy's eyes lit up.

"The guys are waiting," George said with a smile.

"And so's the food!" Bess added.

"What took you so long?" George asked as the girls headed down the beach.

Nancy wrinkled her nose. "I'll tell you after dinner," she said. "You don't want to hear it now, believe me."

"What a day," Bess said, kicking the sand as she walked.

"You mean today?" Nancy asked, surprised.

George burst out laughing. "She sure does! Go ahead and ask her what happened to *her* today."

"I'm never going to model again!" Bess wailed.

"Oh, no," Nancy said. "You saw Doug's painting?"

"You bet I did!" Bess said grimly. "And I almost hit him over the head with it, too! When I think of all those hours I spent posing for that little twerp!"

"I'm sorry, Bess," Nancy said kindly, throwing her arm around her friend. But she couldn't suppress a smile as she glanced over at George.

"I wanted to have a beautiful portrait, like

Diana's," Bess complained, pouting. "He could have used boxes for that painting instead of me."

"There they are," George cried, pointing to three figures on the beach. Nancy felt a tingle of excitement as she saw that Sasha was there, too. She hadn't been sure he would be, and she hadn't felt comfortable asking Bess or George.

"Food's ready," Tommy said proudly as the girls approached. "Best burgers you'll ever eat."

The three couples settled in front of the roaring bonfire, eating burgers and potato salad and catching up on the details of the mystery.

"They let Diana go," Nancy told her friends. "She's going to testify for the state, so they've granted her immunity."

"And I heard Megan gave the *Vanity* to the Nisus Gallery to make up for Bob's thievery. Everyone was talking about the case at Jetstream today," Gary chimed in. "I guess once Megan knew the whole story it was just too painful to keep it."

"So we have a happy ending," Sasha declared with satisfaction. "But who left those notes and warnings for you, Nancy?"

"Bob Tercero did," Nancy said.

"Bob?" Bess asked. "Why would he do that?"

"I guess he thought someone would eventually find out Christopher was dead," Nancy explained. "And he figured if he was helping out with the investigation, he could pin all the blame on Nicholas. But I didn't let him help. And then, when I seemed determined to find Diana, the one person who could tell the whole truth, he panicked and tried to warn me away."

Tommy and Bess picked up the paper plates from dinner.

"So what's the story?" George asked. "What took you so long with Sergeant Jones?"

"I went on a boat ride," Nancy explained. "Remember the old wreck we saw when we went diving? The one right near Nicholas's boat?"

Tommy nodded.

"Well, when Diana told me about Christopher's sea burial, I had a hunch that might have been the boat he was—well, buried in. Nicholas must have gone back to the site to brood. We went out to investigate, and I was right. The police now have all the evidence they need."

"Oh." Bess grimaced. "I'm really glad I didn't have my scuba certification."

Tommy hugged Bess fondly. "Just think, it could have been swarming with sharks."

Bess crinkled her nose. "You are terrible!" she declared, her eyes shining. "If I had been with you, you wouldn't have let the sharks eat me, would you?"

Tommy dropped a quick kiss on Bess's forehead. "No way," he said.

George looked at Gary. "Um, if you guys don't

mind, we'd like to take a walk down the beach," she said. "You don't need us, do you?"

"I've got to get going, actually," Tommy said, rising to his feet. "Bess, walk me back to the jeep?"

The friends said their goodbyes, and Nancy and Sasha were left alone.

"Well, we did it." Nancy lay back on the sand.

"We did." Sasha leaned back next to her, his head propped on one hand. "What a team, eh?"

Nancy smiled, looking at the stars. "What a team," she repeated softly.

"I must tell you, I liked it better when I was the one in danger," Sasha said tenderly. "When I walked into the gallery and found you on the floor—it was not much fun."

"Sasha, I was fine!" Nancy said. "Just a little headache."

"Well, it was not 'just a little headache' when Bob Tercero had a gun at your back." Sasha shuddered. "It was then I realized how important you are to me."

Nancy stole a glance at him out of the corner of her eye. What was he going to say?

"Solving mysteries is a lot of fun, but it can be deadly serious, too," Sasha remarked softly. He reached out and touched Nancy's hair. "Just like being with you."

Nancy caught her breath. She knew he was going to kiss her then, but she couldn't rouse herself to stop him. She *wanted* him to!

He leaned over and kissed her gently, then

with more passion. She could feel his body pressed against hers.

Nancy broke away, her head spinning.

Sasha sat up next to her. Gently, he took her hands in his and brought them to his lips.

"Hey," he said softly, locking his eyes on hers. "Don't you see I love you, Nancy Drew?"

Concluding the Summer of Love Trilogy:

Nancy's summer at the beach is drawing to a close, and the time has come for her to choose between Russian dancer Sasha Petrov and boyfriend Ned Nickerson. But the mystery of the heart will have to wait. First Nancy must penetrate the mystery of Emily Terner, the wealthy executive's daughter who is missing at sea.

Emily disappears with her sailboat off Montauk Point. Nancy finds plenty of suspects—a resentful ex-boyfriend, a rival in the upcoming regatta, and a greedy land developer—but few answers. She's navigating in dangerous waters, and the secrets of the case—and of her love—prove deep and unpredictable . . . in *DEEP SECRETS*, Case #50 in the Nancy Drew Files™.